Their fac⸻s
breath brushed her ⸻

Selina looked at him uncertainly, and Alex at last released her. But when she moved back a pace, he put up his hand and deftly twitched away her scarf. All the carefully hidden hair tumbled free on to her shoulders in a pale, gleaming cascade.

She heard his breath sigh as he took up a few strands, letting them run through his fingers.

''I'd forgotten,'' he said softly ''just how— distinctive a shade it is.'' For a moment, their gazes held, then hers shifted away. ''What did I once tell you it was like?''

''Vanilla ice cream,'' she said, almost inaudibly, and heard him give a slight laugh.

''I thought it was something much more romantic— but I remember now.''

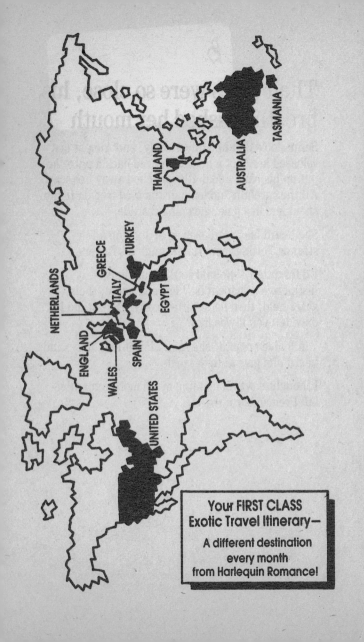

NETHERLANDS
ENGLAND
WALES
ITALY
SPAIN
GREECE
TURKEY
EGYPT
THAILAND
AUSTRALIA
TASMANIA
UNITED STATES

Your FIRST CLASS
Exotic Travel Itinerary—

A different destination
every month
from Harlequin Romance!

LOVE'S AWAKENING

Rachel Ford

Harlequin Books

TORONTO • NEW YORK • LONDON
AMSTERDAM • PARIS • SYDNEY • HAMBURG
STOCKHOLM • ATHENS • TOKYO • MILAN

Original hardcover edition published in 1990
by Mills & Boon Limited

ISBN 0-373-03116-5

Harlequin Romance first edition April 1991

LOVE'S AWAKENING

CHAPTER ONE

'YOU'RE very pale, Selina. Are you all right?'

Ian leaned across the plane aisle to give her hand a quick squeeze and she forced a reassuring smile.

'Yes, I'm fine—honestly. Just a bit tired, that's all. I'll be glad when we get there.'

'Won't we all—especially with this diversion, but we'll be there in——'

He glanced at his watch, just as the intercom crackled and the Greek stewardess announced that they would be landing at Mykonos in ten minutes. Selina exchanged smiles with Ian, but then gently disengaged her hand.

She sighed inwardly. Maybe this trip was going to be even more fraught than she'd naïvely assumed; already, even before the flight was over, what she'd perhaps optimistically visualised as a carefree, amorphous group of young people was busy pairing itself off. As for Ian, his apparently casual friendship was showing every sign of wanting to develop rapidly into something much closer—and that was something she couldn't possibly allow.

What incredible folly had taken hold of her? she asked herself for the hundredth time since going through the departure gate at Gatwick. What madness had whispered seductively in her ear that of course it would be perfectly safe for her to come back to Greece? And yet, was it really so foolish? Surely there was no real danger for her, not even with this last-minute change of route?

Certainly, from the security of the big old house in north Oxford, Greece had seemed a large enough country for her to sneak into for a few weeks at the height of the summer tourist invasion. Lost in the faceless crowds, she would just be one more blonde, jeans-clad, island-hopping sun worshipper—or so she had persuaded herself, with more than a touch of bravado.

But, now that the first sliding lurch of the plane told her that the pilot had already begun his descent, the last remnants of sham courage suddenly oozed away and Greece somehow seemed—smaller, and she more exposed . . . And she hadn't bargained, of course, for the baggage handlers' strike on Crete which had meant their diversion from Heraklion airport to Mykonos, so much further north—so much nearer to *him*.

If her father hadn't been away in the States on yet another lecture tour, she would never have got away with it anyway. But faced with the prospect of a long, dull summer in Oxford—midway through her business studies course—she had jumped like a trout at the fly when Ian, one of her father's classics students, had offered her the chance to take the place, at the very last minute, of a girl who had dropped out of the group spending a sun-and-sea vacation on Crete, to take a fabulously well-paid vacation job in Florence instead.

She'd written to her father, presenting him with a *fait accompli*, and salved her conscience by ringing her aunt, safely out of reach in Cumbria. Aunt Grace had been first appalled, then scathing, then resigned.

'What Edwin will say, I don't know, but I suppose I can't stop you. At nineteen, you're supposed to know your own mind,' though the loud sniff implied otherwise. 'You realise you're taking a dreadful risk, going back there again. I know it's three years, but even so . . .'

Selina had forced a laugh. 'You make it sound as though I'm walking into the lion's den.'

'Well, aren't you?' Aunt Grace's voice was dry.

'But I must go back some time.' It was useless, though, to try to express to her forthright, down-to-earth aunt those strange inner yearnings which just lately had begun, disturbingly, to stir deep inside her, so in the end she only said, 'After all, I *am* half-Greek.'

This time, the sniff was even louder. 'That's as may be. But, mercifully, it's the half that doesn't show. Hmm.' Selina could almost hear the frown reverberating down the wire, then, 'Well, you're obviously determined to go, so just for heaven's sake be careful. Wear dark sunglasses, and cover that hair of yours with a scarf, or something. I don't trust any of them.'

Selina's lips twitched in a reluctant half-smile. *Them* was how her father and aunt, on the very rare occasions when they were forced to do so, invariably referred to all Greeks—and especially to the members of her dead mother's family.

'And most of all,' Aunt Grace wound up, 'I don't trust Alex. I don't know what his game is, but he's been quiet for too long. Your father believes in letting sleeping dogs lie——' like all men, was the unspoken implication '—but all the same . . .'

All the same, Selina thought wryly, as she followed Ian and the others down the aircraft steps into the dazzling mid-afternoon heat, if you could see me now, Aunt Grace . . .

Being forced to fly to Mykonos had been the first shock. She'd worked very hard to convince herself that Crete was practically at the other end of the Aegean from the danger zone, but to find that, instead, they would be catching the ferry for Crete from here, barely half a dozen miles from Tinos, Alex's home island . . . Her shoulders twitched suddenly as though a pair of dark blue, penetrating eyes were boring into her and, pulling the headscarf of heavy white cotton forward so that not one pale vanilla-blonde strand escaped, she ducked behind the bulky forms of two of her group and scurried into the airport building.

The arrivals area was a hot, seething mass of people, and Selina melted into it gratefully. And yet—that uncanny, pricking feeling, the sensation that ice-cold fingers were walking around the small of her back, would not go away. 'By the pricking of my thumbs, Something wicked this way comes——'

For heaven's sake, pull yourself together, she

fiercely scolded that twitchy inner self. It was only the memory of that other nerve-stretching time that she'd spent here, in this very building, expecting at every moment the angry shout, the detaining hand, before, hardly able to credit that she really had escaped, she'd stumbled up the steps into the sanctuary of the London-bound flight.

It was absolutely, totally impossible for anyone to know that she was here. All the same, though, as if seeking the reassurance that she really was safe, she was glad now of the clutch of Ian's hand as he towed her through the crowd . . .

Half an hour later, everyone else had been reunited with their luggage and Selina could sense all too clearly the growing impatience to be off, the urgency to be on board the bus taking them to the ferry.

'Look, you lot go on,' she heard Ian say, his voice not quite managing to hide the irritation which he too obviously felt. 'Tell the driver to hang on while I sort this out.' He turned to her. 'I'll go back through to the Customs section. That KLM flight which came in a couple of minutes after us—your stuff has probably got mixed up with theirs.'

Selina felt hot, tired, her frayed nerves crackling down to her very fingertips—and now this. Dispiritedly, she watched Ian push his way back through the crowd, then backed up against a pillar and stood hugging her arms to her chest, staring down at the tiled floor.

When the hand lightly touched her shoulder she started violently, but then spun round, radiant with relief.

'Ian.'

But it was an airport official—a high-ranking one, to judge by the amount of gold braid that weighed him down.

'Miss Selina Carey?'

'Yes.' She smiled eagerly. 'You've found my luggage. But how did——?'

'If you would just come this way, *thespinis*.' The man's tone was professionally bland and expressionless, but there was—something.

'Is—is there anything wrong?'

But he did not reply, and a tremor of alarm flicked through her, changing rapidly to full-blown panic as, with a sinking heart, she thought, Oh, no, they've lost it. That's what it is. At this very moment, my case is taking off, *en route* for Athens—or Australia, leaving me with just these jeans and grubby white T-shirt that I'm standing up in.

The official opened a door and gestured her past.

'If you will wait here a moment, Miss Carey.' And the door closed behind him with a soft thud. The room was small, just containing a filing cabinet, a couple of chairs and a desk, on which stood—her case and rucksack. Selina reached out to touch them, just to reassure herself that they were not a mirage, then sank down into one of the chairs, weak-kneed with relief.

But her relief was short-lived. If her luggage wasn't lost, why had she been brought here? Could it be some problem with her passport? She was still holding it, and now she flicked it open and took off her dark glasses to study it closely. It was valid for three more years—and there she was, her face, still with the chubby innocence of childhood, staring up at her with the naked vulnerability of all passport photographs. Selina Jane; place of birth—Oxford; date of birth—nineteen years previously.

She closed it and dropped it into her shoulder-bag, then began restlessly pacing around the claustrophobic little room. Her luggage wasn't missing, her passport was in order. So—danger signals flared in her mind—could it possibly be—had one of her group used her as an unwitting accomplice to smuggle drugs through Customs?

With unsteady hands she opened first her case, then her rucksack, but surely both were exactly as she'd packed them the previous evening? She tried to swallow down the blind fear that was rapidly taking her over, but far beneath the wholly understandable panic an even deeper terror was gripping her, numbing her mind.

Ian! Her one coherent thought was that she must get out of this room, back to him and the enveloping security of the group. If she didn't, something terrible was going to happen.

Her luggage all but forgotten, she leapt for the door. The handle turned, but the door would not open. She'd been locked in. Her hand flew to her mouth as she stared down at the handle, then, as it began to move, she backed away, wide-eyed, her knuckles pressed to her lips, as the man came in.

He shut the door behind him, then leaned against

it, his arms folded, as though to pre-empt any escape attempt. He was even more handsome than she remembered. Night after night, she'd seen him, in her nightmares—and her dreams—and yet all those blurred images that had tumbled through her mind like tiny fragments from a child's kaleidoscope had never once come together to make the whole man.

The lean, strong body, the broad shoulders and muscled thighs under the casual beige linen suit . . . the thick, springy, unruly black hair, the deeply tanned face, redeemed from hardness only by the sensitive—*sensual*—curve of the mouth, the perfect aquiline Greek nose, under the fine black brows. And his eyes, almost, not quite, the mirror-image of her own, for while hers were the blue of a placid, sunlit sea, his had the sombre dark of the deep ocean, secret and unrevealing . . .

Those eyes, thickly fringed with black lashes, were watching her now without expression, but still, under that silent scrutiny, her heart began to pound, her stomach muscles to knot and unknot themselves. Good looks, keen intelligence, arrogance—born of being a member of one of Greece's wealthiest families—only just held in counterbalance by dazzling charm, and caustic, not to say razor-edged wit. For a shy, unworldly sixteen-year-old English girl, all those ingredients had fizzed together to make a lethal, overwhelming cocktail, and now . . .

'*Kalimera*. Selina.'

'*Alex?*'

It was a strangled whisper, the voice hardly recognisable as emerging from her own throat. She'd been on Greek soil barely an hour, and here was the man whom, above all others, she'd feared to meet. It was impossible, totally impossible. She wouldn't believe it, and yet, even as her jaw sagged with disbelief, the thought, with horrible clarity, leapt into her mind. Of course, all along, this is what I've known would happen. But even so, of all days for Alex to have come sauntering into Mykonos airport . . . What was that pet phrase of her father's? 'The gods are laughing.' Well, they'd certainly be falling about right now.

She stared at the apparition, still standing by the door. He was not moving a muscle, and yet the threat emanating from him hung in the stifling air, and, feeling the table behind her, she edged round it until it was between them. The oblong of polished wood, narrow though it was, felt solid under her clammy hands, offering her a faint illusion of security.

'It-it's all right, Alex. I don't need your help. I've found my luggage.'

He gave her a brief, though wholly unpleasant smile. 'It seems that I must disabuse you from the outset, Selina. It was I who arranged for your baggage to be temporarily—mislaid, and it was on my instructions that you have been brought in here.'

'*Your* instructions? But that's impossible.'

Even as she spoke, though, she was thinking, What a stupid thing to say. You know Alex well enough to realise that he knows exactly the right person everywhere in this country to ensure that things go precisely the way he wants. And yet, surely, even he . . .?

'You-you didn't arrange the diversion to Mykonos, did you?'

He threw back his head and laughed. 'You flatter me, *agape mou*. But even I don't play games with commercial aircraft. No, I had previously made the appropriate arrangements for your reception at Heraklion.' He lifted his hands in an expressive gesture. 'Your coming here has merely simplified my plans.'

His plans . . . But what precisely were his plans? Ruthless, devious, she had no doubt, like the man himself—and where exactly, she asked herself fearfully, did she figure in them . . .?

'Did you hear me?'

He had been speaking, but she hadn't heard one word. She frowned in puzzlement, then, as his meaning finally penetrated, she felt the blood drain from her face and, as her straw legs folded under her, she collapsed into a chair.

'You——' she licked her dry lips with an equally chalky tongue '—all along, you knew I was coming, didn't you?' she whispered.

'Of course.' He straightened up and came across to lean on the desk, gazing down at her. 'My poor Selina, did you really think that your father could hide you from me? I have known where you were—every day.'

Every day. She shivered at the thought that his

words conjured up: she, hurried back to boarding school by her angry, yet at the same time anxious father, for the first time welcoming the boring routine of lessons, cross-country runs on winter afternoons, evening prep sessions, chapel . . . Then, latterly, back in Oxford, the business studies course, running through the park, late once again for her word-processing class, seemingly as carefree and untrammelled as any of the other students who milled about her. And all the time . . . No, it was unthinkable

'I don't believe you. If you'd known, you would have——' She broke off.

'Come to find you?' He gave her a slanting, cat's smile. 'No. I preferred to wait, to have you drop into my hand like—a ripe peach.' The gesture—a curving of those long, slender fingers around an imaginary fruit—repelled her. 'I was quite certain that one day you would return. But,' there was the faintest glimmer now of a rueful smile, 'you had almost exhausted my patience. And so more positive steps were called for. The girl who withdrew from the group to leave a place clear for you when she was offered that dream job in Florence—the Count and his wife are old friends of mine. Shall I go on?'

'No, don't bother,' she said dully. Aunt Grace, whom she'd impetuously dismissed as fussy and over-careful, had been right. *She* was the fool, and now she was a fly, captured and struggling in the web of Alex's intrigue. But surely, if she fought hard enough, she could break free? After all, she wasn't that timid, malleable sixteen-year-old any longer, and this time she wasn't alone.

Prompt on his cue, Ian appeared as the door burst open, his face almost as red as his T-shirt, and angrily trying to shake himself free of two airport officials. But it was Alex, she could not help noticing, who gave the curt, authoritative command which made them loose their grip and retreat, and the realisation of that made her heart plummet.

Ian scowled briefly at Alex then strode across to her. 'Selina, what the hell's going on?' His voice was loud and belligerent.

'Please, Ian——' she began, then stopped abruptly. *Be careful* was what she wanted to say, but could not. 'Look,' she began again, 'it's all right, honestly.' At all costs, she had to avoid a confrontation between the two men.

'Of course it's not all right. They bring your luggage in here, without so much as a word to you. If we don't get moving, we're going to miss the ferry. And who the hell's this guy, anyway?'

He jerked his thumb in the direction of Alex, who was now leaning indolently up against the wall, though his narrowed gaze was sharp enough.

'Look, Ian,' she said hastily, 'wait for me outside, will you?'

'Wait outside?' He shot another glare in Alex's direction. 'I'm not leaving this room without you.' He put his arm round her shoulders. 'Come on, darling, we'll soon sort this fellow out.'

Selina was not sure whether it was a result of the

arm, the 'darling' or the 'this fellow', but she saw
Alex's fine dark brows snap down momentarily in
an angry frown, before his face took on an
irritatingly smooth look as Ian turned to him.

'Er—*parakalo, kyrie* . . .'

A lift of the brows. '*Boro na sas voithisso*?'

'Oh, don't, Ian,' she burst out, suddenly sickened
by the cruel game Alex was clearly intent on
playing.'He speaks perfect English.'

Ian looked slowly from her to Alex, then at last
seemed to become aware of something of the
tension which crackled in the small room.

'You mean you know him?' he demanded. 'Who
is he, for heaven's sake?'

She could only stare from one to the other, from
Ian's fair, open face, now puckered with
bewilderment, to Alex's, dark and sleekly
saturnine.

At last, she said, 'He—he's my cousin—my
second cousin,' she amended, and sent Alex a
beseeching look, but he merely quirked one dark
eyebrow and clicked his tongue in mock reproof.

'How very remiss of you, Selina. You clearly
have not informed this young man of your true
circumstances.'

He turned coolly back to Ian.

'Permit me to introduce myself. I am Alexis
Petrides. Selina's—second,' there was a light,
mocking emphasis, 'cousin. And her husband.'

CHAPTER TWO

'HUSBAND?'

In other circumstances, Selina thought, with a calmness born of shock, the expression on Ian's face would be comical—almost.

He stared blankly from one to the other, then, 'Is this true, Selina?'

She nodded slightly, quite unable to trust her voice.

'But—how long?' Ian, too, was having problems getting his words out.

'Three years.' It was barely more than a whisper.

'Three? But—but you were only sixteen then. Only a child.'

He swung round accusingly on Alex, who had remained lounging against the wall during this exchange, a half-amused smile playing round his lips. But now he replied coldly, 'It was a perfectly legal marriage if you are implying otherwise. I was not—what is the phrase?—cradle-snatching.'

'But——' Ian shook his head as though to free himself from the bewilderment. 'You've been living in England all that time—boarding school, then in Oxford with Professor Carey. Your father—does he know about this, or was it some kind of crazy, secret marriage, or something?'

'Oh, he knows,' Alex interposed grimly.

She caught his sidelong glance, and her own slid

18

hastily away, to rest on her hands clenched in her lap, the knuckles white under the taut skin.

'I see,' Ian said slowly. 'Well, that's it, then.'

He hesitated a moment, then turned away towards the door as Selina clumsily pushed back her chair.

'Where are you going?'

'I've got a ferry to catch, remember?'

There was a raw anger in his voice which made her flinch. Oh, lord, what a fool she'd been, a blind idiot. 'Please, Ian, try to understand,' she begged.

'Try to understand what? That all this time you've been leading me on you were a married woman?'

'Leading you on? That's not true, Ian—you know it isn't.' She felt desperately guilty, but in the face of the hard-eyed stranger that he had suddenly transformed himself into—and terrifyingly aware of what Alex, silently taking in every word of this humiliating exchange, could make of it if he chose—she had to defend herself. 'You know it's not true,' she repeated softly.

But he threw her a scornful look, then turned to Alex again. 'If she's yours, then maybe you'd better see that she's got your brand on her in future.'

He caught hold of the door, and Selina leapt to her feet, her hand outstretched imploringly. 'Ian!'

She simply couldn't let him go like this, with no explanation. But what could she say? How could she possibly explain, go back twenty years, to when the seeds of disaster—almost like something out of a Greek tragedy, in which the hands of the past reached out cruel fingers to grasp the present—had been sown . . .?

Her father, an impoverished university classics lecturer, already verging on middle-age, obsessed with the dusty, desiccated languages which were the sole love of his life . . . Her mother, Sofia Petrides, from a wealthy Greek family, beautiful, petted, her every whim indulged—except in the one thing she had wanted above all else. When she was sixteen, her adored cousin, Alex's father, had been married off, in an arranged match, with the daughter of an Athens-based shipping magnate.

For years, she had stubbornly refused to marry any of the other entirely eligible Greek males who were paraded before her, and finally having encountered the highly ineligible Englishman on a walking holiday in Tinos, she had married him. Almost, Selina thought involuntarily, as though she wanted to be revenged on the whole of her family—for anyone less like the Petrides males could not possibly be imagined.

But the spark, of defiance on the one side, and—what could it have been? A seeking after youthful passion that had never been known?—on the other, which had ignited between them, had lasted barely long enough for their only child to be conceived. After three years in the cloistered, smothering, wholly alien atmosphere of an Oxford college, Sofia had one day simply disappeared from her daughter's life.

Her father never mentioned her name, and never

allowed Selina to either, and whenever the packages with exotic-looking stamps, containing wildly expensive Christmas and birthday presents, arrived, her excitement had been all but killed by his looks of cold reproof, so that she felt guilty that she should even want to open them. And when Kyria Petrides, her grandmother, had written, formally inviting the twelve-year-old Selina to spend the summer holiday at the family villa on Tinos, the first reaction of both of them had been a blunt refusal.

But, surprisingly, it was Aunt Grace who had put her foot down. Selina had overheard drifts of the conversation, 'But you must let her go, Edwin. After all, like it or not, they are her relatives, and the fact that Sofia behaved so disgracefully doesn't alter the fact that she's her mother.' She didn't catch her father's low reply, but then her aunt had laughed and said something about, '. . . nothing to worry about . . . far too sensible for that . . .'

And so, in the care of the Olympic Airways stewardess, Selina had flown off to the Aegean, to all the exotic, vibrant colour and heat and noise, and had met her 'other' family—the dark-eyed woman whom she barely remembered as her mother, all the exuberant, extrovert cousins. And Alex . . .

The quiet, self-contained, rather plump little English girl had been wholly unprepared for the totally overwhelming impact of it all, and the whole summer had been a disaster—almost, but not quite as great a disaster as that second visit, four years on . . .

'Well?' Ian was looking at her coldly.

But she shrugged wearily, her hand falling back limply to her side. 'Oh, it's all too complicated.'

He nodded, then, without looking at her again, opened the door. 'Bye, Selina.'

She made a small, involuntary movement after him, but Alex, swift as a cat, moved across to her and slid his arm around her waist, imprisoning her to his side.

The moment the door had closed, though, she broke free from his grip and turned away to look out of the dirty window. Seconds later, she caught an oblique view of Ian, hurrying across the tarmac to a waiting bus. A couple of young men from their party were hanging around its steps, and as she watched, a curious light-headedness detaching her from all emotion, he said something to them. One appeared to be expostulating, gesturing towards the airport building, but then they all scrambled up the steps as the bus began to move.

She watched it pull away, until it disappeared from her line of vision, then thought, still in that curious, detached way, I'm not really here. It's all a bad dream, and all I have to do is screw my eyes up tight, like this, and I can wish everything away.

'If you are quite ready, Selina?'

'But—where are we going?'

'Home, of course.'

'Home?' she echoed faintly.

'To Tinos.'

Tinos. Nearly three years on, but just the name was enough to conjure up images of the past . . . the Villa Ariadne—the spacious, rose-pink Venetian-style house, surrounded by cypress trees and rolling, grey-green olive groves, and filled with the laughter and vitality of an overpoweringly ebullient Greek family.

She moistened her lips nervously. 'They—they won't all be there, will they?'

'But of course.' Alex spread his hands, as if in apology, but she could not miss the gleam of chill amusement in his eyes. 'Where else would they be at this time of year? Your grandmother demands it of us all.' He paused, then added drily, 'What's the matter, Selina? You are very pale.'

The same words exactly as Ian had used on the plane, though she was almost past feeling the irony of that. She could only think: her grandmother . . . all the others . . . how would they receive her, after what had happened, what she'd done?

'I-I'm not coming with you,' she said in a small, high voice. He regarded her across the desk, his dark blue eyes narrowing slightly. 'But you have no choice.' She could hear the thread of steel. 'This time, you will obey me—in everything. And if you force me to carry you out of here you will regret it very much—later.'

The fear was leaping through her like a brush fire now, almost out of control, but somehow she had to hide it from him. Summoning from somewhere deep inside her a spirit she hadn't known she possessed, she set her soft chin at a defiant angle.

'That's quite ridiculous, Alex, and you know it. If I choose to pick up my things and walk out of here this instant, there won't be a thing that you or any of your gold-braided minions,' she hurled the word at him, 'can do about it.'

'Oh, but I'm sure you wouldn't be so—foolish, as to try,' he said silkily, though the steel was still there. For a moment she stared up at him, nonplussed, then, not quite confident of what her next but one move would be, she shot him a scowl and took a firm hold of her case.

Instantly, his hand gripped hers to wrench it free, and with an exclamation of pain she withdrew it sharply. She measured the distance to the door, then decided that other tactics were needed.

'You surely can't mean to take me to Tinos against my will—to kidnap me?' Her laugh sounded forced, though, even to her own ears, and she shot him an appealing look in a desperate attempt to tap the reservoir of affection that, once upon a long time ago, he had felt for her.

But then, when he did not reply, she asked woodenly, 'Just how long do you intend to keep me there?'

'Oh, until——' he gave her a cat's smile '—until I choose to let you go.'

'You'll never get away with it, Alex, never. My father will——'

'Your father!' he cut in brutally. 'Your father, *agape mou*, is in no position to interfere in my affairs any longer. In any case, have you forgotten, he is away in California at present?' So he really had been keeping close tabs on them. She went even paler, but before she could reply he continued, 'You still do not seem to have grasped the situation. I could have had you brought back here at any time in the last three years, had I chosen, and your father—whatever he may have told you—would have been quite powerless to stop me. Now that you have been so—unwise as to return, he is even more helpless.' He paused. 'I am your husband, and it is *my* wishes that you will obey.'

Despite her inner turmoil, she forced herself to meet his gaze defiantly. '*Your* wishes? Oh, no, I——'

'And what precisely did that so charming young man mean, about your leading him on?'

'I——' she began, then broke off. One part of her was telling her that there was no need at all for her to justify her actions—however innocent—to this man. But another, more cautious part, was urging her at least to set this particular record straight.

'No, Alex, whatever Ian says, I swear I didn't encourage him . . .' Her voice trailed away miserably for a moment, as she remembered Ian's set, angry face. 'I promise you, I've never forgotten that I'm your w-wife.'

'Oh, come now, *koukla mou*, surely you've been trying to forget that small matter since before the wedding feast was over—or have you forgotten that?'

She bit her lip. 'No—no, I haven't. But can you really blame me—for the way I behaved?

Everyone pressurising me, my father away at that summer school in Canada, rushed into it before I really had time to think. I was only sixteen, remember,' she went on, with a spurt of anger, 'or have *you* forgotten *that*?'

'No,' he said, regarding her sombrely, 'I have not forgotten.'

'My grandmother, my mother, practically on her deathbed, you—all of you begging me to——'

'Oh, no, Selina,' he intervened coldly. 'You must know that it is not in my nature to beg—and I certainly did not *beg* you to be my wife.'

'But you could have stopped it. *You* weren't a child. You were twenty-six—the head of the family.' He shrugged carelessly, but she went on, 'And it was just for the sake of your precious *family*—because my mother and grandmother wanted it.'

In his frown she caught a fleeting glimpse of the arrogance of the Petrides male. 'I do not do anything—and least of all, marry—merely to please others.'

'But—but why me?'

She looked up at him helplessly, in her mind seeing again all those glamorous, sophisticated young women whom she had watched through that fateful summer, some subtle, some blatant, but all making a set at Alex, and all making her feel like that plump, gauche twelve-year old all over again.

He did not reply, but gave her an odd little smile, then took her hand and, turning it, lightly brushed across the palm with his lips in the softest of kisses.

The butterfly touch burned her skin, sending a strange prickling sensation like pins and needles up her arm, but as she went to snatch her hand away his hold tightened.

Looking down at her slender fingers, he said thoughtfully, 'Yes, I think that young man was right, in one thing, at least. I shall have to put my *brand* on you from now on.'

With a feeling of helpless fatalism which would have done credit to Cassandra, prophetess of doom, she saw him produce a tiny box from his jacket pocket. He flicked it open with his thumb-nail and she saw—her wedding-ring. As she watched, a rabbit mesmerised by a snake, he took it out.

'Give me your hand.' His voice now was devoid of any emotion, but when she instinctively thrust her hands behind her back he snapped angrily, 'Don't play games, Selina!'

Without a word, she held out her hand, but as he went to slide the ring over her finger the panic rose in her again and she flinched away. With a half-smothered expletive, he clamped his other hand over her wrist and fiercely rammed the ring over her knuckle. It went on much more easily this time, she thought involuntarily, for *then* her hands had still retained their slight childish pudginess.

She stared down, seeing for a fleeting instant not the wide band of heavy antique gold—made, like all the Petrides wedding-rings, from the huge nugget which Christos Petrides had found in the Klondike in 1849 and brought home to Tinos when he returned to claim his bride, and which was kept now in the vaults of the bank in the Platia Syntagma in Athens—but past that, to that other day, when Alex, his hands not quite steady, had slipped it on to her cold finger. A day which had taken on such a strange, surreal quality in her mind . . .

The family—her grandmother's smile of quiet triumph; her mother, already marked for death, almost too ill to attend the ceremony, but with eyes which glowed in her grey face; the tiny, white-washed chapel in the villa grounds, the high, sweet singing fading away to nothing, somewhere beyond the circle of small, golden candle flames; the scent of flowers; the priest's glittering vestments; the gilded icons which gazed down at her with softly gleaming eyes . . . Until even that faded, and it was just the two of them: she, like an obedient wax puppet—and, after all, that was exactly what she'd been, in her grandmother's fabulous silk wedding dress, the bodice encrusted with pearls—and Alex . . .

Alex! Her head jerked up, but he was frowning abstractedly at the ring. Face to face with him again, she was forced to wonder fearfully, for the millionth time, how he would have borne the blow. Such an intensely proud man, and the Greeks set such store on keeping face, didn't they? Even though the family must have instantly closed ranks—for the marriage, and her flight, had seemingly remained a secret—he would inevitably have been very, very angry with her—and still was, with an anger which had festered for three years . . .

She swallowed convulsively, and the movement must have sent a tiny ripple through her body, for he glanced up. Their faces were so close that his warm breath touched her mouth.

As she looked at him uncertainly, he at last released her, but when she moved back a pace he put up his hand and, sliding a finger into the knot of her scarf, deftly twitched it away, so that all the carefully hidden hair tumbled free on to her shoulders in a pale, gleaming cascade.

She heard his breath hiss, then, as she forced herself to stand docilely, he took up a few strands, lifting them and letting them fall from his fingers.

'I'd forgotten,' he said softly, as though at least half to himself, 'just how—distinctive a shade it is.' He looked from her hair, directly at her, and for a moment their gazes held, then hers shifted away. 'What did I once tell you it was like?'

'Vanilla ice-cream,' she said, almost inaudibly, and heard him give a slight laugh.

'I thought it was something much more romantic, but yes, you are right—I remember now.' He turned away abruptly and swung her luggage off the table. 'Come.'

She hesitated for one final moment, then picked up her shoulder-bag and followed him out through the door, her head in the air, her stomach fluttering somewhere down around her knees.

Instead of going back through the main arrivals hall, though, he led her through a side door and out into the burning heat, where drawn up just outside was a black Mercedes, its boot already open and a

young man at the wheel. He got out, took the cases
and tossed them into the boot, while Alex handed
her—and never was there a truer word, she
thought, half fearfully, half resentfully, feeling the
vice-like grip of his fingers around her
elbow—into the rear seat, then slid in beside her.

The two men kept up a lively conversation all
the way to the harbour, but Selina, unable to follow
a word of it, and conscious that she was under
almost constant, frankly curious scrutiny in the
driving mirror, huddled herself further into the
corner away from Alex, and stared out of the
window, stony-faced.

The car purred to a halt on the quay. The young
man unloaded her luggage, shook hands with Alex,
said something, at which they both laughed and
which she was uncomfortably certain was closely
connected with her, nodded a polite '*Herete*' in her
direction and roared off.

There was a powerful-looking motorboat pulled
up alongside the quay, and Alex picked up her
cases, lowered them on to the deck, then jumped
lithely on board. As he did so, a loud blast from a
ship's funnel made her swing round and she saw a
large, white-hulled boat easing away from the
dockside. Among the gaggle of passengers leaning
over the rail, she caught a glimpse of a shock of
fair hair and a red T-shirt. Ian! It must be the
Heraklion ferry. For one crazy second she thought
of running along the quay to hurl herself across that
slowly widening gap, but she was too late, and, in
any case, Alex would never let her get away a

second time.

He looked up at her, holding her gaze for a moment, as though he had read her thoughts, then stretched out his hand, but she ignored it and scrambled on board. Before she'd even plumped herself down on the narrow slatted bench, he'd started the engine and was manoeuvring through the harbour, which was crammed with expensive-looking sailing boats of all shapes and sizes, towards the open water beyond.

Selina slumped on the bench, leaned her elbows on the rail that ran along the side of the boat, and gazed morosely back at Mykonos Town, quite indifferent to the beauty of its gleaming white houses, ranged all over the hillside like a giant child's building blocks casually flung down. Gradually, the ribbon of water behind them widened and deepened to blue-black, their wake spreading like ripples of white lace, and staring down, almost mesmerised, at that frothing line of water, only half hearing the soft hiss of each wave against the hull, she saw again in her mind her last journey across this same stretch of sea . . .

In the few days between the betrothal—after she'd finally succumbed to her mother's increasingly urgent pleadings—and the ceremony, Alex had been very correct with her, kissing her just once, on the cheek, a formal, cousinly kiss, his cool lips barely brushing her skin.

Except that one occasion though—her breath quickened at the memory. She'd been nervous and on edge all day, and had ended up going downstairs far too early for dinner, so had wandered out into the deserted garden. Through the dusk, she'd seen Alex coming towards her, but before she could escape he'd taken her hand and steered her along a path among the cypresses at the back of the villa.

Behind his casual conversation, she'd sensed an inner tension which had transmitted itself from his hand to hers and from there to the whole of her body, until she'd felt herself almost twitching with nervous apprehension, like a cat before a thunderstorm. The path had narrowed so she'd been able to disengage herself and was walking on ahead when the dinner gong sounded. With a gush of relief, she'd turned—and cannoned violently into him. The next moment, his arms were round her and he was pulling her to him.

'Selina.' His voice was thick, and she'd felt herself trapped against his hard body. Then, as he'd lowered his head towards her,

'No!' With a gasp that was all but a shudder of revulsion, she'd torn herself free and blundered past him, back to the security of lights and people on the terrace.

By the time Alex had appeared, rather pale and with his lips compressed into a taut line, the meal had been half over. After that, she'd seen him so seldom that she'd been quite convinced that he was avoiding her.

But then, at the wedding feast, seated beside him at the enormous table on the vine-shaded terrace, she'd been, as in the chapel, conscious only of him, everything else—the laughter, the lively conversations, the clinking of glasses, servants passing to and fro with yet more food—fading away into a blur. Then, as he'd leaned across to speak to someone sitting further down the table, his arm had suddenly brushed her arm, his leg, hard and well-muscled, had moved against her leg.

Simultaneously, they'd both turned to each other and she'd seen, in those marvellous dark blue eyes, that same quickly igniting spark. He'd wiped the look away immediately and replaced it with the former cool, impersonal expression, but she'd sat motionless, her hands crushed together in her lap under cover of the white tablecloth, the fingertips biting savagely into her damp palms as she fought herself for composure, while the smiling, laughing faces seemed to close in on her, leering, and Alex's dark, brooding, familiar face turned suddenly into a menacing satyr's.

But then she'd stumbled to her feet, mumbling an incoherent apology, and hurried into the house. Even as she'd opened her bedroom door, she'd had no idea of what she intended to do, and only went through to the bathroom to splash her face over and over with cold water, her eyes carefully avoiding that wild-eyed stranger in the mirror.

Back in the bedroom, she'd stood quite still in the middle of the floor for several minutes, and then, quite suddenly, she'd begun ripping off the silk dress, trampling it to the floor in her haste. She'd pulled on a skirt and blouse, dragged her case from the wardrobe, tearing clothes from their hangers and flinging them in anyhow. As she'd fumbled in her shoulder-bag to check that her purse, passport and return ticket—a ticket that, just a few minutes before, she'd thought she would never use—were safe, a gust of laughter from the terrace below had made her freeze, but the house itself was silent.

She had been just easing open the door when she'd caught sight of her wedding-ring. She'd stared down at it, strange feelings warring inside her, then wrenched it from her finger and placed it, with exact geometric precision, on the centre of her dressing-table.

Clutching her case to her, she'd fled down the back stairs, expecting at any moment to feel a hand roughly seize her shoulder and she'd forced herself to tiptoe, breath suspended, past the noisy, saucepan-clanging kitchen, then had gone flying through the olive groves and out on to the road to Tinos Town. Even then, she hadn't been able to stop running, and when the tourist moke, filled with young Germans, had pulled up beside her, she'd almost cried out in terror.

They had dropped her off at the harbour, but the ferry to Mykonos had just left. She'd stood, staring after it, and something of her frenzied anxiety must have transmitted itself to a middle-aged English couple on a yacht, for they'd called across to her that they were just leaving for Mykonos, and if she wanted a lift . . .

A sudden spurt of salt spray blinded her for a moment. She jerked her chin away from the rail and looked round at Alex. He'd taken off his jacket, and she could see his powerful arm and shoulder muscles, tensed as he gripped the wheel, steering towards the rapidly approaching land. His black hair, slightly over-long, exactly as she remembered it, was curling into the neck of his white cotton shirt.

Alex . . . Why hadn't he chased after her? She'd asked herself that question so many times, but even here she was no nearer an answer. He could so easily have caught up with her, either on that agonisingly slow sail to Mykonos, or at the airport. And if not there, why hadn't he followed her to England? She'd certainly expected him to, had lived in dread of the inevitable furious confrontation between him and her father.

But gradually the fear had receded. Her father certainly had been furious at first, at least as much with her as with 'that Petrides clan', and he'd talked angrily about getting an immediate annulment. But then his innate caution had reasserted itself, his perpetual belief that if a problem was ignored for long enough it would go away, and he'd done nothing, telling her that there would be time enough to sort things out in the future.

And so it had stayed a secret, shared only with Aunt Grace, and she'd returned to school, still Selina Carey. In the normality of school life the whole episode had almost taken on the nature of a shifting, ephemeral dream, barely more than a heightened version of the exaggerated stories her friends told of their holiday romances.

Inescapable reality had asserted itself just once, a few weeks after term had begun, with a brief letter to her father to the effect that Sofia Carey, formerly Petrides, had died. After Selina's enforced marriage and flight there had, of course, been no question of her—or her father's—attending the funeral, but even so, for weeks afterwards she'd cried herself to sleep, weeping for the lost relationship with her mother that might have been but which never could be now . . .

She realised that the engine had stopped, and, lifting her eyes from a whorl of varnished planking which she'd been studying unseeingly for at least ten minutes, she saw that they had arrived. Ahead of them, was the small, pine-fringed cove which she remembered so well, just a narrow strip of pale gold sand lying between the water and the sombre green of the trees, while through the thick foliage on the hillside above she could just make out the blur of rose-pink among tall fingers of cypress trees.

Alex let the boat drift in until its side rasped gently against the wooden support of a small jetty, while she sat very still, only her hands fidgeting endlessly with the clasp of her bag.

'Let's go.'

He was standing over her, so without a word she got up awkwardly, but then a wave of dizziness swept through her, so that she stumbled against him. He caught her by the arm, then tilted her face up towards him, his lips tightening as he registered her extreme pallor.

'Don't look like that, *koukla mou*.'

'L-like what?'

He gave a wry smile. 'As though you are about to be fed to the lions.'

'Walking into the lion's den . . .' At the faint echo of her own unthinking words, her whole body gave a convulsive start, and he sat down on the bench seat, drawing her down with him.

'Selina.' His dark eyes were very serious. 'You must stop looking like this—like a defenceless, hunted animal. No one is going to say a word to you about—what happened, I promise you. It is all forgotten.'

'Of course it isn't,' she burst out wildly. 'How could it be?'

She tried to free her hand, but he kept a tight hold of it.

'Well—perhaps it isn't forgotten, but *nothing*,' for a second she glimpsed the despotic assurance of the head of the Petrides family, 'will be said. You know,' his eyes narrowed reflectively, 'if you go on in this melodramatic way, I shall begin to think that you feel guilty about the whole affair.'

'Actually, I do.' Her overwrought nerves put a snap into the words. 'I feel guilty for ever having let myself be talked into the stupid charade.' She quailed at his expression, but plunged on, 'And, for your information, I've d-despised myself ever since for being so weak. So if you think I——'

'Be quiet.'

He spoke very softly, but momentarily she was disconcerted, then, 'No, I won't. Let me ask you this: I left you once. What makes you so sure I won't do exactly the same—disappear, I mean—the moment I get the chance?'

His fingers tightened roughly on her hand, as though he would like to catch hold of her and shake her, but all he said was, 'You know, my sweet, you were exasperating when you were twelve, and it seems to me you are even more exasperating now.' He eyed her thoughtfully. 'I shall simply have to make sure that you do not get the chance to—disappear again.'

In spite of the heat, she suddenly felt icy cold at the silken thread of menace in his voice.

'Now, come.' And he pulled her to her feet.

CHAPTER THREE

THEY walked up through the pine woods without speaking, the only sounds the crickle-crickle of the cicadas and their footsteps crunching on decaying pine needles. Selina knew perfectly well that Alex had deliberately chosen to shroud himself in silence, but she still found it totally unnerving. Every time she gave him a swift, sideways glance, though, his frowning profile was so forbidding that she immediately gave up any idea of brittle conversation. And besides, the climb was so steep that, even though he was carrying her luggage, she gradually fell behind, hot and panting.

The pines thinned out at last into the olive grove. The first time she'd come to Tinos, this place had held a childish fascination for her. She'd loved the gnarled grey trunks, the twisted branches, and on hot afternoons she'd sometimes sneaked off here with a book, grateful for the solitude and the silence.

There'd been one tree in particular, a very old one—it had been so much her favourite that the family had jokingly called it Selina's tree. Alex had found her there one day and told her that people said it was a thousand years old, and she'd often sat under it, propped against its rough trunk, or lain on a rug, watching the sunlight filtering down through the moving lacework screen of its silver-grey leaves and tiny fruit.

'What's the matter?' He'd paused, waiting for her to catch him up.

'Oh, I was just looking for that old tree. You remember, the one I used to like so much. It was just over there, wasn't it?'

'It died two winters ago,' he said briefly.

'Oh, no—I'm sorry,' she said huskily, then, horrified, felt her eyes fill with tears. She knew that his penetrating gaze was on her, and turned away, angry with herself. Crying for a tree, for heaven's sake.

'But we took a cutting from it, and planted it in its place. Look—there it is.' He pointed to where a small, sturdy sapling stood, then added casually, 'It seemed a pity to let Selina's tree die.'

'Oh.' Caught completely off guard, she could only stare at him across the width of the path, but his face was inscrutable in the dense shadow, and after a moment he walked on, leaving her to follow.

The olive trees washed round the villa lawns like a grey-green sea, and from behind a tangled screen of flowering shrubs came shrieks and splashes. The swimming-pool—they'd all be there. Almost without realising it, she edged up closer to Alex, her heart pit-patting wildly. He said nothing, but, gripping her arm tightly, he led her quickly across the rough, sun-parched grass on to the shady terrace.

Mercifully the patio and entrance hall were deserted, though a pair of small, damp footmarks led in a trail across the geranium-red quarry tiles and away down a passage. She followed him up the stairs then, without thinking, turned towards the small bedroom she'd occupied on her previous visits.

Alex, though, went on along the uneven, winding passage to the back of the old house, where, at the far end, a window was open, letting in a thread of cool air from the hills behind the villa. He opened a door and gestured her past him. The closed shutters made the room a cool, twilight cave, but then he half opened one of them. She glanced round quickly, then, seeing a pair of men's jeans slung down on a chair, black espadrilles kicked off beside it, her mouth went dry and she backed away from him, blundering into a chair.

'This is your room, isn't it?'

He nodded. 'That's right.'

Of course. How naïve she'd been—where else would he have brought her? Momentarily, her eyes slid to the huge double bed, which was covered in an embroidered brown and cream counterpane in coarse cotton, then skittered away in confusion.

She glared at him defiantly. 'Well, I'm not——'

His lip twisted slightly, but all he said was, 'I didn't imagine you would. At least,' he paused long enough for maximum effect, 'not yet.' His meaningful look made the colour pound in her cheeks as he went on, 'But you *are* staying in my wing of the house. I've had my old dressing-room prepared, through here.'

A large, old-fashioned bathroom led off his bedroom. Unwillingly, she followed him through it, then he opened another door at the far end and they were in the room at the angle of the house. It was small, with tall shuttered windows on two sides, and was simply but attractively furnished with a single bed, a pine chest, dressing-table and wardrobe.

He dumped her case on one of the brightly patterned wool rugs. 'This is your room. At least, until . . .'

He left the sentence unfinished, and she turned away, making a great deal of putting her shoulder-bag down on the dressing-table.

'By the way,' he continued, 'it might have escaped your attention, but I'm afraid you have to share my bathroom. However, we can come to some amicable arrangement, I've no doubt.'

Her eyes flew to the door and, horrified, she saw that there was no key, no lock, even.

'And you might also not have noticed that the only way in and out of this room is through my bedroom.'

She stared at him, her lips tight. So she was a prisoner, and Alex was her gaoler—and she could do nothing about it. A feeling of sick helplessness was creeping through her, paralysing her active mind into lethargy. This time, she knew, there could be no escape . . .

He regarded her for a moment longer, then nodded slightly, as if satisfied with the obvious effect of his words.

'Your grandmother wished to see you as soon as you arrived, but I think perhaps you need a few minutes to prepare yourself.'

When the door had closed behind him, she felt her way across to the bed, her eyes still fixed rigidly on the panels, as though expecting him to materialise through them, then dropped down, seconds before her legs gave way.

She was dreaming—she had to be. It was another of those nightmares she'd had for months after her flight but now when she savagely bit on the soft inner flesh of her mouth the pain was all too real. What was she going to do? The question hammered at her brain, but then she thought, with surprising calm, Wash your face and comb your hair. If Alex came back and she wasn't ready, he'd be angry.

She'd only ever seen him really angry once, when Nikos, his younger brother, already under a ban for reckless driving, had 'borrowed' his new Aston-Martin sports car, and had written it off against a brick wall. But the seven-year memory of Alex's fury still made her mouth run dry . . .

In the bathroom, she splashed her face and wrists with cold water. She desperately wanted a cool shower, but she'd already registered that there was no lock on the bathroom door either, and, even though she could catch no sound from Alex's room, she dared not strip off.

As a tiny show of defiance, she hadn't intended to change, but on reflection a grubby T-shirt and jeans would give *them* a distinct advantage, so back in her bedroom she opened her case, pulled out the first thing she saw—a simple, short-sleeved dress in dark, Provençal-print cotton—and dragged it on.

She threw herself down on the dressing-table stool, her fingers all thumbs as she fumbled for her comb and began tugging it through her long silky hair, impatiently at first, but then, as usual, the sensuous feel of the soft strokes of the comb soothed her like a cat. She laid the comb down at last and got up, smoothing her dress and slowly surveying herself in the half-light. Long-legged, high, rounded breasts, gently curving hips. . . She'd never be eligible to join the ranks of the Willowy Blondes, but at least that adolescent podginess, which she'd shed rivers of tears over, had, in the end, disappeared almost overnight.

And she did hold herself well, she thought dispassionately. All those old-fashioned deportment exercises, with Gibbon's *Decline and Fall* on her head, and the games mistress roaring, 'Head *up*, Selina, chest *out*, bottom *in*.'

Her face stared back at her, as pale as her hair, the small delicate features taut with apprehension, her wide blue eyes darkened almost to the colour of Alex's.

From the corner of her eye, she caught a faint movement and saw him behind her, reflected in the mirror, watching her. She swung round.

'You ought to knock.'

'I did, but you were too busy admiring yourself.' His voice was calm, level, but beneath this her sharpened senses caught the faintest stir of something else. Anger? No—not that, she thought, with sudden, flaring panic . . . And the expression in his eyes, which she'd caught fleetingly, only increased her sense of vulnerable isolation.

She took a deep breath to quell those butterflies and said simply, 'I'm ready.'

Back along the passage in silence, the only sound the creaking old boards, down another staircase, then finally Alex knocked at a door.

'*Peraste.*'

For one moment, Selina had the wild idea of running, but then Alex, with a quick squeeze of her arm which was meant to be either a warning or reassurance—she was unsure which—was ushering her into the room.

'Selina is here to see you, Thia Eleni.'

And even as her eyes strained to accustom themselves to the shuttered dimness, he had gone . . .

Methodically, Selina pulled the brush through her silky hair. Well, it really hadn't been so bad. Rather like one of those dreaded visits to the dentist when, in spite of her terrors, she hadn't needed a filling after all.

Her grandmother could not have been more gracious. She'd warmly kissed her erring granddaughter on both cheeks, enfolding her in a fragrant cloud of Balenciaga, pressed on her some of the pink sugared almonds from the pretty little papier mâché box which she always kept by her for all the younger members of the family, seated her on a low stool to study her, and finally patted her cheek with a bejewelled hand, pronouncing that she was even prettier than the last time she'd seen her.

And that was all. That was the nearest she'd got
to any accusations, much less reproaches. In fact,
a bemused Selina had emerged feeling vaguely like
Alice in Wonderland tottering out of the rabbit
hole. Alex was right. He'd told her that nothing
would be said, and it was apparently true. All her
dreadful misdemeanours—her running away and,
even worse, her staying away—which must have
shocked the entire Petrides family to its rigidly
respectable Greek core, were to be ignored, to
remain firmly under the carpet as though they'd
never happened . . .

A knock roused her from her reverie—a knock
which said, I'm knocking, but only because I
choose to and, in any case, don't keep me
waiting—and Alex came into the room. He had
changed, but only into cream canvas jeans and a
pale lemon cotton shirt. Of course—she'd
forgotten that after the formality of their lives for
most of the year, the younger members of the
family always dressed casually at the villa, so her
simple scoop-necked dress in lime-green cotton
jersey which she'd bought for those lively taverna
evenings with the group in Crete would after all be
quite suitable.

She did not turn round, but stared at him in the
mirror, the brush suspended above her hair, as he
crossed the room to stand right behind her, looking
down at her. As though she were someone else, she
watched his eyes travel slowly over her reflection,
taking in the curves of her breasts and hips in the

pretty white cotton lace bra and panties, then she saw the scalding blush break out all over her body.

She longed to leap to her feet, snatch up the blue crinkle cotton housecoat which she'd so unwisely dropped on the chair a few minutes earlier, and clutch it to herself. But she cringed inwardly at the thought of the mocking smile this would provoke, so she had to content herself with just edging forward so that his trousered leg no longer brushed against her bare back, prickling the fine golden down on her skin.

So far, since Alex had captured her at the airport, she'd felt exactly as though she'd been treading water, desperately keeping herself afloat. But now, meeting that equivocal regard in the mirror, she sensed suddenly the unseen currents tugging inexorably at her, threatening to drag her under to her destruction. She simply couldn't turn to meet his gaze head-on, and even the reflected Alex was all at once too much, so she transferred her attention instead to her hairbursh, dragging a finger across it, slowly, so that each bristle sprang stiffly back from under her nail.

'Are you ready?' he asked abruptly. 'Dinner will be served in a few minutes.'

'Y-yes, just about. I'll come through to your room, if you'd like to wait there.'

But he ignored the heavy hint and instead sat down on the bed, remarking casually, 'Thank you, but I prefer to stay.'

She flung down the brush and leapt up, snatching at the dress, which lay across the bed beside him.

But it was trapped, intentionally or otherwise, by his leg.

'Excuse me,' she said through her teeth, and wrenched it free.

Turning her back on him, she dragged the dress roughly down over her head and shoulders, then started violently as she felt the light touch of his fingers against her back as he deftly closed the long zip. She willed herself not to attempt to resist as he slowly turned her to face him, fixing her eyes on the third button of his shirt, but then froze as he lifted her hair away from the neck of her dress and let it fall to her shoulders in a shining curtain of pale silk.

At last, he put his thumb beneath her chin, tilting her face up to his, studying it quite dispassionately for long moments, before he murmured softly, almost as though he was speaking to himself, 'You had the promise of great beauty at sixteen, Selina *mou*, and now that promise is more than fulfilled.'

As she gaped at him, her blue eyes widening, he gave an odd, rather strained smile. 'At twelve, you were appalling. Fat, that wonderful hair scraped into two ugly pigtails, a brace on your teeth, and your clothes . . .'

He rolled his eyes expressively and, with a spurt of anguish she remembered those white cellular cotton shirts, the beige shorts, the *sensible* brown sandals which her father's elderly housekeeper had bought for her . . .

Teased beyond bearing by her new, exotic cousins, and by one in particular—the raven-haired

Cleo—she'd taken refuge one day in the olive
grove, sobbing quietly into her knees, until Alex
had found her. He'd been coming up from the
beach with his latest girlfriend—a beautiful,
sophisticated creature who had seemed like a
goddess to Selina's tear-soaked eyes—but he'd
peremptorily dismissed the pouting goddess and
sat down beside her, putting his arm round her and
insisting that she tell him what was wrong.

She hadn't really been able to put it all into
words, of course, but he'd finally gathered that one
small part of it was her despised wardrobe. He'd
briskly ordered her to dry her eyes, then whisked
her off—alone—in his boat, to Mykonos and the
most chic boutique in town. As they'd arrived back
in Tinos harbour, her eyes like stars, her hands
clutching the tissue and gold string-wrapped parcel
which contained her new peach-coloured T-shirt
and shorts, the swirly daisy-flowered skirt, and,
best of all, the pretty bright pink sun-dress, he'd
swung her up on to the quay and smiled warmly
down at her. 'Better now?' Unable to trust her
voice, she'd only nodded, then, as a sudden burst
of adoring gratitude had swept away her shyness,
she'd hugged him convulsively, telling herself that
she would love her lordly, grown-up second cousin
forever and ever . . .

From somewhere below, a gong echoed softly
around the house.

'Dinner,' said Alex.

He stood up, holding out his hand to her, and she
allowed herself to be led from the room.

CHAPTER FOUR

THE long trestle-table was set up, just as Selina remembered it, under the vine and bougainvillaea-shaded terrace. Most of the family were already there, and a lively buzz of conversation struck Selina as she hovered uncertainly in the doorway. Simultaneously, Alex's hand was in the small of her back, propelling her unwilling legs forward, and the animated chatter stilled, so that in the sudden silence she was absolutely sure that the whole family must be able to hear her heart bounding erratically against her ribs.

Among the bewildering array of second, and even third cousins, looking round at her, there were some faces she recognised. Her grandmother, of course, at the head of the table, resplendent in black silk and pearls ... Sonia, a softer version of Alex, her younger brother, with her husband, Demetrios ... and those must be their two teenage sons, much more grown-up than she remembered ... and, there, sitting sedately between her mother and father, Poppi, the pet of the family, who'd been a baby the last time Selina had seen her, and was now a lovely, dark-eyed little girl in a white smocked dress ... Thia Katrine, Selina's great-aunt, whose fiancé had been killed in the civil war and who had never married, still in black mourning forty years on ...

Alex's mother was not here, of course. When his father had died, she'd severed all ties with the family and now spent her summers in a yacht anchored off the Côte d'Azur. She hadn't even come back for their wedding . . . At the far end of the table, though—that must be Thios Stefanos, her mother's elder brother, his elegant wife, Calliope, and their daughter Cleo—yes, she remembered Cleo, her arch-tormentor, until Alex had stepped in. How old was she now? Twenty-five, surely—four years younger than Alex—and even more beautiful, with her raven-black hair and gleaming tan, stunning in a simple—deceptively simple, Selina amended silently—white dress, chunky gold jewellery glinting against her throat and slim wrists. Selina's eyes met Cleo's black ones, and all at once she was the gauche twelve-year-old schoolgirl again . . .

Alex must have felt the tremor which ran through her whole body, for momentarily the pressure of his hand hardened and he pushed her out ahead of him. Once more, she sensed that air of authority—acquired no doubt from having had to take over as head of the family at far too early an age after his father's premature death—and she could almost feel the waves of silent command exuding from him. Just one word out of place, that's all, he was warning all of them.

As if in response to that unspoken threat, there was a polite chorus of '*Kalispera*, Alex, *kalispera*, Selina*,*' then, as she sank into the chair which Alex pulled out for her, grateful for the warm, apparently genuinely welcoming smile of his sister beside her, half a dozen conversations rapidly broke out again.

Alex slid into the seat beside her, his leg brushing past hers, and she edged away a little, then he began a lively exchange with his brother-in-law. The classical Greek she'd studied at school—and been coached in by her father—was sufficiently close to the modern idiom for her to get the gist of the conversations that began to flow around her, and, in any case, whenever anyone addressed a remark to her they were at pains to use their normally impeccable English.

But for most of the time Selina, her nerve-ends twanging like overstretched violin strings, and horribly aware of the surreptitious, even if carefully veiled glances which were surely swirling around her head, kept her eyes on her plate, quite incapable of speech.

Somehow, she chewed, and even swallowed some of the delicious *fetta* cheese soufflé that was placed in front of her, though its delicate richness was turning to powdery ashes in her throat.

'*Oriste*, everybody.' A young man, in faded denim shorts and black vest, bounded up the terrace steps behind them. 'Selina, darling.'

Before she could duck, he had seized her, dragged her to her feet, and was planting a smacking kiss full on her lips. Behind her, she heard her grandmother's stern voice. 'You are very late, Nikos.'

Nikos—Nik—Alex's younger brother, obviously even more exuberant than ever. He released her at last and shot his aunt a quite unrepentant grin. 'Sorry, Thia Eleni,' and he dropped into the only vacant place, directly opposite Selina.

She had just subsided back into her seat and was forcing down another mouthful of soufflé when, across the table, she heard Nik remark cheerfully to the table at large, 'What's on the menu tonight? Fatted calf, I presume.'

Just for once, Selina was quicker on the uptake than Alex. She shot him a swift sideways glance from under her lashes and saw him frowning at his brother, then her grandmother said frostily, 'What do you mean, Nikos?'

'Well, surely—it must be fatted calf, to celebrate the return of my beautiful prodigal sister-in-law?'

There was a soft intake of shocked breath around the table, but Nikos did not appear to notice. Selina was certain that there was nothing malicious in the remark—on the contrary, he was only, in his inimitable way, trying to say, 'Welcome back', and at the same time to lighten the tension that hung over the whole terrace. But even so, her hands clenched on her knife and fork. . .

'And what can we look forward to later?' Nik was continuing, quite unabashed. 'Humble pie, I suppose.'

Selina, crimsoning with mortification, heard a faint giggle—from Cleo, she was sure.

'That's enough, Nik.'

Alex had not raised his voice, but she heard the distinct crackle of ice just below the surface.

'Or am I too late? Have they made you eat it already, Selina *mou*?'

'Nikos.'

Alex had still not moved a muscle, but Selina, almost writhing in her chair, quivered at the barely suppressed fury in his tone, and Nik, after exchanging one long look with his brother, hesitated, then finally closed his mouth on whatever further indiscretion he was about to produce.

Instead, he launched into a vivid account of an emergency appendectomy he had witnessed the previous week at the teaching hospital in Athens where he was studying. Although the blood-curdling description was clearly in danger of putting the rest of the family totally off their *garithes pilafi*, the aromatic mounds of spicy prawn pilaf which had been set down on the table in two huge pottery dishes, Selina sensed that they were happy, even grateful, to give him full rein now that he was finally off the taboo subject of her return.

The rest of the meal passed with agonising slowness, but by the time the delicious dessert of *baklava*, with its honey-soaked layers of light-as-air pastry filled with walnuts, at last arrived, she had managed, with the aid of a glass of light Greek white wine, to summon enough spurious poise to exchange a few bromide sentences with Sonia. But she knew that she would be quite incapable of sitting through what was bound to be the even more leisurely ceremony of coffee and liqueurs and got clumsily to her feet.

Without daring to look at Alex, she blurted out, 'If you'll all excuse me, I'm very tired.' And then, amid a murmured chorus of '*Kalinikta*, Selina', she thrust back her chair and made her escape.

Back in the cool darkness of her room, she sat on the edge of her bed drawing in, one after the other, long, shuddering breaths in a futile effort to calm herself.

The family had clearly learnt their lesson well, obeying to the letter Alex's stern injunctions—except of course for the irrepressible Nik—but even so, she simply couldn't stay. It would be utterly disastrous, in every way, if she did. She would leave—tomorrow. Of course, she would tell Alex. This time she wouldn't run off in that cowardly, underhand way, but she *would* go—and he would understand. However angry he might be, surely his pride would not allow him to detain her by force?

She stared tensely at the window, every sense magnified by the darkness, expecting at any moment to hear the sound of his bedroom door opening, and then the door to her room. But all she heard, for a long time, above the wild, thumping beat of her heart and the distant crick of insects in the olive grove, was the gentle tinkle of cups drifting up from the terrace, the low murmur of conversation, among it the unmistakably deep timbre of Alex's voice.

He'd obviously decided that she really was exhausted and, clearly having no fear that she

would attempt another disappearing act, had
sufficient tact to leave her alone tonight. She would
have preferred to tell him right away, while her
resolution was at white-heat, but it would have to
wait till morning.

In the meantime, the torpor of fatigue really was
beginning to creep through her mind and body in
a grey tide, so that she could barely hold herself
upright on the bed. She washed perfunctorily,
nervous of spending long in the shared bathroom,
then flung on her pink, flower-sprigged cotton
nightie and collapsed into bed.

The olive trees shushed softly in the warm breeze
and beyond them the sea lapped at the
pebble-edged beach. Below, on the terrace, the
quiet ebb and flow of conversation was now
strangely lulling . . .

She woke with a violent start, her mouth dry with
sudden panic, then lay staring into the darkness.
The house was wrapped in silence, but something
must have disturbed her; an owl, hunting in the
olive grove perhaps—or Alex, come upstairs at
last.

She lay for long minutes, staring at the
communicating door, and knew that she would not
settle again until she was sure that he was safely in
his room. She climbed out of bed, and, her
heartbeat stopping at each creak of the floorboard,
tiptoed across to the door and stealthily opened it.
No light showed, no sound came, although the faint
sandalwood scent of cologne hung in the air, and

she was almost certain that she could hear faint, regular breathing.

Expelling her own pent-up breath in silent relief, she closed the door again, got back into bed and turned over, pulling the sheet up around her shoulders—and then she froze.

A dark shape was seated on her dressing-table stool, its shadowy bulk silhouetted against the pale half-circle of glass.

'W-what are you doing here?' She sat up, clutching the sheet to her.

'I did not intend to disturb you.'

'Then why did you come?' Distrust—and raw fear—put a sharp edge to her voice.

There was a soft gleam of white teeth in the darkness.

'Does a husband need a reason to come to his wife's bedside?'

'N-no, of course not. At least . . .' She floundered to a halt as she heard him chuckle quietly.

'Don't worry, *koukla mou*, I'll leave you to sleep undisturbed in a very few moments.'

He uncoiled himself and crossed the room towards her, then, before she could slide away under the sheet, he had sat down beside her. Taking her by the shoulders, so that she could feel the warmth of his hands striking through the thin cotton to her own cool skin, he very gently drew her towards him.

His lips, as they met hers, were warm, his kiss at first gentle and undemanding on her closed mouth. Gradually, though, under the sensuous slide of his skin against hers, the scent of him, her taut mouth involuntarily relaxed, and at that treacherous, minute weakening of her defences he slid his tongue between her lips, far inside the moist warmth of her mouth, teasing, caressing it into surrender, gently persuading a response from her that she was desperately willing herself not to give.

But it was no use—all she could taste and feel was him, and dimly she heard herself give a faint moan. She could feel one of his hands at the nape of her neck, tangling in the long silky strands, while the other moved to take hold of her chin, his fingers splayed against her tender flesh, so that she could feel the pulse flicking just beneath the surface of his thumb.

It was that erratic pulse that saved her—the lightning realisation that Alex was not nearly as cool and poised as she had thought him. In fact, far from it—she could feel now the spark of desire kindling in him and she drew back her head sharply, pushing frantically at his chest. Never before had Alex kissed her like this, and, as she felt those swirling currents dragging at her again, the panic flared in her.

'No—no, Alex, don't.'

But he still held her to him—so tightly that she could feel the irregular pounding of his heartbeats—for long minutes, before finally releasing her.

'It's all right, *koukla mou*.'

He might have been soothing an overwrought child, awakening from a nightmare, but under the calmness she heard the not-quite-steady breathing, and a husky throb which terrified her. He took her hand and, holding it between both of his, raised it to his lips, very softly kissed the palm, then set it down.

'Goodnight, Selina.'

She felt him tense to get up. 'No, don't go yet, Alex.'

'No?'

'I—I must talk to you,' she added quickly, afraid that he would misunderstand. In fact, she desperately wanted to be alone, but much better to tell him now than wait until morning. After all, she wasn't going to sleep again tonight—she was quite certain of that. 'I can't stay, Alex,' she blurted out. 'I'm leaving tomorrow.'

He said nothing, so she went on disjointedly, 'It's all a terrible mistake. You must see that. It was a mistake last time, and it still is.'

Still he did not reply, so she added, a note of pleading in her voice, 'Please try to understand. I was just too young.'

'Yes, you are right.' Alex's sombre voice came from the darkness. 'In that, at least, we misjudged—you at sixteen were not at all like a sixteen-year-old Greek girl. And I agree that you were subjected to what some might call unfair pressure—emotional blackmail, even—being called upon to comply with your mother's dying wish.'

'But why,' she faltered, 'why did she so desperately want me to——?'

'To marry me?' There was a touch of wryness in his voice. 'You may find this difficult to believe,' the wryness was even more evident now, 'but she honestly thought it was for your own good. She knew, of course, that she was dying and I think she wanted to bequeath you into my protection.'

'Into your protection? But I was already in the care of my father. I had been, remember, ever since—ever since she left us both.'

'Yes.' He was speaking very gently now. 'But you must know how she felt about him. And she wanted desperately to break you free from his influence over you.'

Selina stiffened with anger, but before she could respond he went on, 'When you came out here three years ago, we all saw that you had changed. You'd been an inhibited, withdrawn child—you'd become a rigid, buttoned-up young woman, afraid of your beauty, of your body, terrified of your natural feelings. We could see that you were in danger of being warped for life, of being turned into a bloodless replica of your father.'

The colour blazed across her cheeks. 'My father! You don't know him, so——'

'No, but your mother did.' She flinched at the cold contempt in his voice. 'And so, when you so happily told her of his future plans for you, of how he had already set up a job for you in the library of his own college——'

'But I'm not doing that. I didn't want to.' In fact, going out and enrolling on the business studies course had been the first spark of independence she had shown in her whole life.

'We were not to know that. And it seemed to me *obscene* that a beautiful young girl should be entombed among shelves of dusty old books, like the princess put to sleep forever in the glass coffin, just when she was on the brink of womanhood.' He paused. 'Your mother seemed to think that marriage to me would be your salvation.' She caught the note of self-deprecation, but was not able to respond, and he went on urgently, 'Selina, she did care for you—love you very much.'

'Oh, yes.' She could not bite back the bitter retort. 'So much so that she walked out on me when I was two.'

'And how much guilt did she endure for that, do you think, for the rest of her life, for the choice she made—between you and the lover who refused to be encumbered with a young child?'

As Selina gazed at him in sick horror, he went on gently, 'Yes, it is true. Your father has clearly shielded you from the whole truth, but now that you are no longer a child, it is time that you knew.'

When Selina was still silent, lost in the maelstrom of her thoughts, he continued quietly, 'You must realise that her own tragedy began when she too was sixteen, when she was prevented from marrying the only man she ever loved. I think she wanted us to marry in the hope that you would love me as she had loved my father, and he had loved her.' He paused, but she was quite unable to reply, her fingers plucking convulsively at the sheet. 'You must understand, Selina, that she loved my father so passionately that, in our marrying, she saw a final healing of that terrible wound within herself.'

She didn't want to—*couldn't* think of that, wouldn't allow herself to see the traumatic event of her marriage in this new perspective. And, in any case, how could Alex talk of love in terms of their own arranged, loveless match? So she only repeated stubbornly, 'But it was still wrong of her. She shouldn't have done it—and you shouldn't have agreed. I *was* only sixteen.'

'But you are not sixteen now.' Behind the irritation there was a soft *frisson* of sensuality, so that her busy fingers instinctively clutched on the sheet. 'And now that you are older, you can surely make up your own mind and, if you wish, withstand such pressures. Besides, I promise you, there will be no family pressures this time.'

But wasn't Alex 'family'—twice over? Her second cousin—and her husband. And surely there would be inexorable pressure—overt or more subtle—from *him*. . .?

'Yes, I can make up my own mind now, and that's why I'm leaving—tomorrow. I—I don't love you, and——'

'Love?' he broke in harshly. 'What has love to do with it? You know that your mother did not love your father. Do you think your grandmother loved the man who was chosen for her, or that my mother loved my father?'

'No, but——'

'And just where, as a matter of interest, do you intend going? To rejoin your little friends in Crete?'

'No. Back to England. I shall go to Daddy's—to my solicitor's, to start annulment proceedings.'

'On what grounds?'

She was grateful for the darkness, for she could feel the hot blush spreading over her whole body. 'Non-consummation. My—my father said that the marriage can be set aside——'

'And just when did he say this?' There was a chill in his voice now—and something else, which unnerved her even more.

'When I first got back.'

'And has he said so since then?' Still there was that something.

'Well, no,' she admitted reluctantly. 'But in any case,' she injected a note of defiance into her tone, 'I'm old enough now to look after my own affairs. So——'

'And I suppose you are also planning to repay the dowry.'

Her head jerked up. 'Dowry? What dowry?'

'Oh, did your father forget to mention it?' he said silkily. 'How very remiss of him.'

'But there was no dowry,' she said in bewilderment. 'How could there have been? Even in Greece, dowries—if they're still given at all—are given *by* the bride, not to her. Even I know that,' she wound up more confidently. If he was trying to confuse her, he hadn't succeeded.

But Alex ignored her words. 'I, of course, did not want a dowry,' the arrogance in his voice set her teeth on edge, 'but your mother and grandmother insisted that everything was done correctly, in the old way. And so, between them, they provided the dowry for you.'

She frowned in puzzlement. Nothing of this had been spoken of to her in the days leading up to the wedding. But, after all, she'd been nothing but a puppet, had she?

'In that case, don't worry,' she said coldly, 'there'll be no need for you to repay me—and Grandmother won't want you to either, when she accepts that it's best that we part.'

'You miss the point completely, my sweet.' She felt rather than saw his unpleasant smile. 'I already have repaid it. Two days after you so precipitately left, I sent it after you.'

Her bewilderment was total now. 'But I don't understand. There must be some mistake.'

'No mistake, I assure you,' he responded grimly. 'The money was lodged in your father's bank account in Oxford within forty-eight hours.'

Selina stared at him through the darkness, her eyes dilating. She had no doubt now that he was speaking the truth. But why had he done it? What a foolish question. Knowing Alex as she did, he had made the gesture in utter contempt for her and her father. And yet, why had her father never told her of it? Certain that Alex was relishing her dismay, she struggled to pull herself together.

'In that case, we—I will repay the debt that we owe you,' she said resolutely, though at the thought of her meagre bank balance she almost shuddered.

'You think so?'

'Of course.'

'You really think you will be able to repay me?' His voice was very soft now.

'H-how much is it?'

'One million pounds.'

'One million——! But that's impossible.' The words were jerked out of her.

'I promise you.'

'I don't believe you.'

'Are you doubting my word?'

She had to, otherwise . . .

'One million pounds was your mother's estimate of your worth. Do not forget that, whether you like it or not, you are a Petrides.'

The hauteur in his voice was proof enough.

'Well, the money will still be intact. It won't have been touched.'

'Are you quite sure of that, Selina?'

'Yes, of course I'm sure,' she said indignantly. 'What do you think we are? Thieves? We may be poor, in comparison with you lot, but——'

She broke off abruptly, almost choking with the anger, not only for herself, but for her father. But then, quite suddenly, the indignation, the righteous anger which had swelled within her burst like a pricked balloon. Horrified suspicion darkened in her mind, turning instantly to horrified certainty.

The move, within weeks of her return, from the college rooms to the beautiful Edwardian house and garden . . . the antique furniture . . . the books . . . the prized marble head of a Greek youth which adorned her father's study . . .

When she'd asked, he'd said, with a hesitation

that she'd put down to his natural embarrassment, that her mother had left him a bequest in her will, and she'd accepted this gladly, thinking that her mother had been trying to cross the bridge to him in death which she'd been unable to cross in life. There'd been no more talk of annulment. Her father had told her, for the time being, to leave everything to him. And so she had, she thought grimly . . .

Her heart sank into black despair. How could he have done it? And how would they ever pay Alex back? Well, for a start, they'd just have to sell the house. And that Greek head—at least prices for property and antiques had leapt up in the last couple of years . . . She set her soft lips in a line of steely determination.

As if he was reading her thoughts, Alex said carelessly, 'Do not upset yourself. The money is of no account.'

'Maybe not to you, but it is to me.' Through her despair, anger was rising, washing through her like bile. 'I've been handed over, sold, hands tied, like an animal at market.' But then the despair rose again, driving back the tide of anger. 'A million pounds—how can I ever repay you?'

'Oh, there are many ways, I assure you.' That husky throb was back in his voice and she felt him gently lift a silky strand of hair with one finger. 'After all, Selina, you are a woman any man would be proud to have as his wife.'

But I don't want to be your wife, she wanted to scream at him, but instead she only said woodenly, 'All of this changes nothing. I'm still leaving tomorrow.'

His fingers tightened momentarily on her hair until she gave a stifled whimper of pain. 'You are not leaving tomorrow.' She sensed that he was keeping his voice even only with a tremendous effort. 'Not tomorrow, or any other day—until I choose. And I would not advise you to try. We too have learnt our lesson well from your last foolish escapade—I should warn you I have given orders that you are to be watched. Every second of every day.'

He got up and she felt him looking down at her. 'And as for the nights—well, we shall have to see.'

CHAPTER FIVE

WELL, Selina had been right about one thing, at least. She'd had a sleepless night, only dozing into a dream-racked half-slumber as daylight was already edging through the closed shutters . . .

Selina reached across the table for an orange from the wicker basket of fruit, peeled it, cut it into exact quarters and sucked the sweet juice listlessly. The only thing to be grateful for was that she was alone on the terrace. The family, if they took breakfast at all, tended to take it late at the villa, but even so they had all long since finished, leaving empty coffee-cups and the remnants of half-eaten bread rolls.

She took up a small bunch of seedless green island grapes and leaned back, but then, as a slight movement in the garden below caught the corner of her eye, her lips tightened. That gardener—still in the same spot, still hoeing those same scarlet geraniums to within an inch of their lives . . . Just as, when she'd finally emerged from the bathroom into Alex's bedroom, she'd found one of the maids on hands and knees busily beeswaxing the already gleaming floorboards.

'I have given orders that you are to be watched every second of every day.' The softly spoken warning—steel veiled in silk—echoed in her ears. There was going to be no Houdini-like escape this time, and she might as well get used to that fact. And, in any case, if she did get away, back to England, there would be the inevitable confrontation with her father.

How could he have done it? She asked herself the question for the hundreth time. And for the hundredth time she cringed with shame at the thought of the contempt which Alex had surely felt towards them for three long years. Of course, her father *was* weak; she wasn't quite sure how old she was when she first became aware that the childhood idol had feet of clay. But *she* wasn't weak—not now, anyway.

Somehow or other, however long it took her, she was going to repay the money—every penny of it. For until then, it remained blood money, a price on her head, a gigantic link in the chain that bound her unwillingly to Alex. All at once, she realised that she was convulsively twisting round and round on her finger the gold ring that he had forced on to her just the day before, and she jerked her hand away.

In this nightmare situation, she was totally alone. Her father had betrayed her, and the Petrides family, for their part, had all conspired against her—— She caught herself up with a slightly shamefaced grin. Oh, come on, you're starting to sound like the last act of a Sophoclean tragedy—or at any rate you're well on the way to developing paranoia.

But was she? Certainly, on all sides, she'd been deceived and manipulated. But that had been three years ago. She was a different person now—a different person, even, from the girl who'd flown off to Greece barely twenty-four hours earlier. She was nineteen, and from now on she was going to run her own life. No one was going to manipulate her ever again, even—*no*, most of all, Alex.

'Would you like more coffee, Kyria Petrides?'

The young girl, carefully setting down the coffee-pot at her elbow, made her start.

'And, when you are ready, Kyrios Alexis said you are to come down to the beach.'

Oh did he? Selina smiled her thanks at the girl, while resolving instantly to spend the entire day in the olive grove, or better still, closeted in her bedroom. She sat, watching the maid retreat along the terrace, and abstractedly flicked her knife against the edge of her plate. *Kyria Petrides . . .* The new title gave her a peculiar, rather unpleasant feeling, like snagging a broken nail on nylon. It was as though Selina Carey was beginning to slip inexorably away, her identity merging in Alex, to become one of his possessions—a Petrides possession, she added silently.

She couldn't get away, that was obvious—at least, not until Alex chose to release her. But he was not a patient man, and what patience he did have would, sooner or later, run out, and surely then he'd finally accept that he had to let her go? And the best way to ensure that, she thought with clinical coldness, was to keep their marriage to the empty sham that it was now, and not give him that final hold over her.

But then, quite suddenly, she felt again the touch

of his hands on her shoulders, of his lips pressed against hers, his tongue probing the warm moistness of her mouth . . . What would it be like, do you think, to be really held by Alex, caressed by those slender fingers, *made love to* by him . . .?

The insidious thought had slid up from the depths of her subconscious and she thrust it away angrily. Don't be such a weak, spineless fool, she told herself fiercely. If once you give way to him, if you allow him to make this marriage a reality, you're lost. You're making your own decisions from now on, remember? And that includes choosing your own husband. Get this shell of a marriage dissolved, just as soon as you can, and then when—no, *if* you ever marry again, you must love the man *you* choose, and he must love you.

She gulped down a final cup of strong, fragrant coffee, got up, then stopped, leaning against the table and chewing her lip in urgent thought. Maybe she would go down to the beach, after all. If she did sulk up here all day, Alex—and the others—would guess that she was hiding herself away, just as she had done when she was twelve—and would feel once again that blend of pity and contempt that she had always dreaded, but until now had not had been able to counter. She would face them, and start, as from now, her waiting game with Alex, and they would just have to see who tired first.

She was running lightly up the stairs to change when a thought went through her, lightning swift, and she stopped dead, clutching the banister, her throat dry. Alex wouldn't—*couldn't*—take her by force—could he? Surely, his pride, if nothing else, would hold him back from inflicting that ultimate degradation on her? And yet, what were his parting words last night? 'As for the nights—well, we shall have to see . . .'

Through the wooden stair-rail she caught the eye of the maid, now industriously sweeping the hall tiles, and, much more soberly, she went on up to her room.

Even before she reached the bottom of the winding path, she could hear the shouts, and when she emerged from the welcome blue-green shade of the pines into the dazzling heat she saw that two tall posts and a net had been set up on the soft creamy sand and a boisterous game of volley-ball was in progress. Alex's two teenage nephews pitted against him and, she registered with a little spurt of some feeling she could not quite identify, Cleo.

The boys gave her a cheerful wave, Cleo ignored her, but Alex threw the ball down on to the sand, temporarily halting the game, and sauntered across to her. As he approached, she turned her back, dropping her bag, and shook out her black and white beach towel then knelt down, smoothing it out with careful deliberation.

She did not look round, even when she heard his footsteps crunching softly on the sand. Only when, out of the corner of her eye, she saw his bare, tanned legs right beside her, one all but brushing her thigh, did she slowly straighten up.

In spite of herself, her eyes flickered over him, taking in the hard, pared lines of his body, so clearly revealed beneath the old white T-shirt and brief, chopped-off blue denim shorts, slung low over his lean hips and straining across his flat stomach.

'*Kalimera*.' It came out ungraciously. She could not quite meet his eye, and this made her angry with herself.

'You took your time.'

His casual tone sent sparks flying from the nervous irritation smouldering inside her. She pushed her sunglasses further up her nose and scowled straight up into his dark eyes.

'Of course, it never even occurred to you that I might not leap to obey your command, did it? That I——'

He lifted a careless shoulder. 'Of course not. Why? Should it have done?'

'——that I might have preferred to do something else this morning.'

'Like hiding yourself away in the olive grove, you mean?' His tone was not pleasant. 'Well, that at least would have been quite like old times, wouldn't it?' He regarded her coolly for a few moments. 'I was going to ask if you slept well, but you obviously did not.'

'Of course I didn't,' she snapped. 'You made very sure of that before you left.'

His frown could almost have been innocent perplexity. 'I'm sorry. Was it something I said?'

Her lips tightened, but before she could think of a retort she became aware of the two boys, flopped on the sand, and watching the little husband-wife cameo with undisguised curiosity, and Cleo standing, impatiently tossing the ball from one hand to the other.

'Your *partner* wants you, I think. Don't let me keep you from your game.'

And, as she saw Alex's mouth thin to an angry line, she dropped down on to her towel and began rummaging through her bag, as though he had already gone. She heard him mutter something under his breath, then he turned on his heel, scuffing up little spurts of sand, and walked back to join the others, peeling off his T-shirt as he did so and hurling it to the ground.

As soon as the game restarted, though, Selina dropped the suntan lotion she had been clutching and sat up, her chin on her knees, an unwilling yet compulsive spectator. Alex was at the net and, as she watched, his long, lean body was put at full stretch as he reached for the ball, high over his head, the muscles flexed tautly under the smooth, burnished skin. With a grunt of triumph he snatched it out of the air and sent it crashing down on to the sand at the far side.

Even from that distance, he exuded a physical allure wholly animal in its unconscious athletic grace, and as she gazed raptly at him she felt her own breathing growing increasingly fast and shallow, heard the blood pounding in her head.

'Alex.'

The intense shock of hearing her own voice say his name aloud jarred her back to reality. She jerked her head sharply, as though someone had struck her, and as her breathing slowly steadied she wrenched her eyes from him to take in again the other players, all of whom had for a few moments ceased to exist.

Cleo, she realised, had discarded her emerald-green beach wrap to reveal quite the skimpiest bikini she'd ever set eyes on—two minute scraps of emerald for a top, and a narrow-thonged G-string below. Presumably, her grandmother never made it to the beach, Selina thought sardonically. What she would have made of Cleo's almost bare breasts—and almost bare everything else—she could hardly begin to imagine. Funny—she'd always thought that Greek girls did not flaunt their charms too liberally, but no doubt the gorgeous Cleo was a law unto herself.

She stared at the other girl for a few moments longer, then suddenly leapt to her feet, unbuttoned her own turquoise towelling wrap and threw it across her bag. Then she looked down at the matching glistening wet-look bikini that she'd bought in her frenzied last-minute shopping expedition in Oxford. She'd been slightly worried that it was too revealing—weren't they all, this year?—and that had been for the group on Crete. Now, she felt very shy all at once at the thought of such an alarming amount of bare flesh being exposed to Alex's dark blue gaze . . .

On the other hand, though, now that she studied herself for the first time since trying it on in the store, she could see that it did suit her—the

unstructured top and wide-apart shoulder straps set
off perfectly the high fullness of her breasts, while
her slim waist and the long, graceful, feminine
curve of her hips and thighs were delicately
emphasised by the high-cut leg.

All she needed was a good tan. She carefully
rubbed in some of the high-factor sun-lotion which
she'd brought to protect her fair skin, at least for
the first few days, took off her dark glasses, and
flopped back. The sun and the tops of the pine trees,
swaying gently to and fro in the hot breeze,
combined to make a dazzling pattern of gold
against her closed eyelids. She felt the intense heat
drive through her skin, far into her body, seeking
out all the little deep knots of tension, dissolving
them, until she lay totally relaxed, drifting off,
blissfully oblivious now of everything, even finally
the volley-ball game a few yards away . . .

When the shower of cold water droplets hit her
skin, she sat up with a smothered gasp, to see Nik,
in navy swimming trunks, shaking the water off
himself like a dog.

'Oh, Nik, go away!' she exclaimed in
exasperation.

'Sorry, Selina.'

He grinned broadly at her, but then, as he flopped
down beside her, they heard Cleo's triumphant
shout, 'We won, Alex darling!'

Quite unable to tear her eyes away, Selina
watched as the girl wrapped herself around him.
Well, at least he was making no attempt to return
her kisses—but then, he wasn't making much

effort to disentangle himself, either, she thought sourly.

She glanced at Nik and realised that he was watching her closely, but then, as the two boys ran off down the beach and into the water, he sprang precipitately to his feet, pulling her up after him.

'Come on, Selina. We'll show them.'

'Oh, no, Nik, please——' she began, but he was already towing her determinedly across the hot sand.

Alex finally disengaged himself from Cleo's embrace and stood, watching them approach. As Selina neared him, she saw that his eyes were solely on her. His expression was enigmatic, but all at once she wished, far too late, that she had not discarded her beach wrap.

'Selina and I challenge you to a match!' Nik exclaimed. 'Don't we?' he added, turning to her.

'Well . . .' she hesitated.

'Perhaps Selina doesn't *play* volley-ball.' Cleo's eyes were on her, coldly assessing the situation. 'Maybe you should have asked her first, Nik.'

'You do, don't you?' He turned to her.

She knew just how a cornered rat must feel. Her gaze went slowly from Cleo's black, insolent stare to Alex's coolly inscrutable, navy-blue regard and the old panic welled in her. She'd never played volley-ball in her life, and this match certainly wasn't the one to learn on.

She made a small, involuntary movement to turn away, caught the gleam of malicious triumph in those black eyes, and heard herself say, 'I haven't played much, but sure—that's if you don't mind doing most of the work, Nik.'

She smiled warmly at him and, although she did not even glance at Alex, none the less she felt him imperceptibly relax.

At first, it was a nightmare. She missed almost every shot, so that Nik had to scurry about the entire court, covering for her, and she lost them point after point as her arms and legs steadfastly refused to react to messages from her tense brain. Even the easy shots, which she was quite positive Alex was deliberately feeding to her, ended up in the net or way beyond the base-line.

And then, as she stretched despairingly for a spinning ball from Cleo, she stumbled and went headlong on the sand. As she slowly picked herself up, she thought suddenly, This is ridiculous. OK, I've never played the stupid game in my life, but I *was* captain of netball and lacrosse, and senior girls' tennis champion, wasn't I?

In fact, when she'd returned to school three years ago, she'd thrown herself frenziedly into sport for the first time, discovering to her own astonishment that she had a natural aptitude for ball games. And yet now, here she was, allowing the tensions and hang-ups of that podgy twelve-year-old to tie her once more into awkward, ungainly knots.

Brushing the sand off herself, she took a deep breath. 'Ready.'

Cleo served to her, high and wide, but she reached out and smashed it back over the net at her opponent's feet.

'Oh, good shot, Selina.'

Alex's shout made her glow with pleasure just as she'd always done when she was a child at a single word of praise from him, but then the glow faded. After all, why should she allow herself to be so grovellingly grateful for one crumb of congratulations from *him*?

Gritting her teeth determinedly, she served to him, then struck his return fiercely out of reach. Suddenly, the match had changed character. It was no longer a carefree beach game; it was much more—a needle contest, each side silently striving for victory. Alex and Nik were both good—very good—players, but Cleo, Selina now realised, was far too busy making graceful stretches and leaps designed much more to show off the curves of her body than to keep the ball in play.

Gradually, the gap in points was narrowing, and Cleo, her frustration beginning to show, began to play her opponent, not the ball. Several times, the hard missile came straight at Selina—never Nik—and finally struck her hard on the shoulder. Well, she thought grimly as she rubbed the tender spot, if Cleo really wanted to play it that way . . .

During the next point, with the scores even and each side needing just two points for victory, Selina for the first time, used the powerful two-handed chop, perfected after long hours on the practice courts for a vital inter-house tennis match, but just as effective now, and sent the ball straight at Cleo. Somehow, though, Alex intercepted and returned it, but with her next shot Selina, angry now with both of them, smashed it into Cleo's midriff.

'Ow, that hurt.' As Nik guffawed with laughter, Cleo scowled under the net at her. 'It's against the rules, and you damn well know it.'

'Oh, I'm sorry Cleo.' Selina's voice dripped honey. 'I didn't realise. I was just, well, following what other people seemed to be doing.'

And Cleo, her face an unbecoming dull red beneath her tan, threw her a killing look and took her place again.

Match point. As Selina prepared to serve to Alex, she caught in his eye a gleam of what just might have been secret amusement. Suddenly, all her pent-up frustration and anger—with herself as well as him—exploded in her brain and went into the serve that she hurtled at him. With his lightning reflexes, he just managed to reach the ball and fist it back, but Selina surged forward to return it.

The other two had faded—they were just blurred figures on the periphery—as each struggled for supremacy. She sensed that now, for the first time, Alex was eager to win as she was, and this fed her determination that this was one battle, at least, that she would not lose to him. He was driving her further and further back from the net—it was now or never. She brought up both hands and, with all the power in her body, put a vicious edge of spin on the ball, killing it on the sand at his feet.

'*Thavma*, Selina!'

With a cry of triumph, Nik swooped on her and swept her off her feet, then whirling round, kissed her jubilantly. Selina, her own jubilation effervescing through her veins like champagne bubbles, laughed out loud and kissed him back.

But then, as he swung her higher over his head, the laugh died abruptly on her lips when she caught sight of Alex, his own congratulatory smile quite faded, standing motionless on the sand, hands on hips, watching them, his face an angry storm-cloud.

She wriggled down through Nik's arms just as he ducked under the net and came up to them.

'Well played, both of you,' he said, lightly enough, but his eyes, holding hers, were cold.

'Yes, I reckon we make a pretty good team,' Nik chipped in. 'Don't you, Cleo?'

The girl did not reply. Instead, she turned away with an abrupt toss of her black hair, snatched up her beach wrap and stalked off up the path towards the villa.

They watched her go in silence, then Nik said, 'Dear, dear, we are in a mood today. Anyway, I'm boiling. Let's have a drink.' He gestured towards a cool-box in the shadow of the pines.

'Not just now, Nik,' Alex replied evenly.

'How about you then, Selina?'

'No.' Alex had spoken softly enough, but something in the word froze her to the spot.

'The drink can wait.' He held out his hand to her. 'Come for a swim—now.'

But she didn't want a swim—she wanted a long, cold drink. She was on the perilous brink of open defiance when she caught the warning in his eyes.

'Just a minute, then. Wait while I pin my hair.'

Alex walked across with her in silence, leaving Nik to head up to the pines. With hands which she realised irritably were not quite steady, she fumbled in her bag, finally dug out a blue plastic clip and caught up on to the top of her head the plait into which, for coolness, she had tied her heavy hair before coming down to the beach. All the while Alex watched her, his silence becoming increasingly oppressive.

She straightened up slowly, but then, as she still hesitated, he gripped her wrist and led her off down the beach, his fingers digging cruelly into the soft flesh.

'Let me go, Alex. Y-you're hurting me.' Her voice trembled, less from the pain, though, than from her sudden fear of this bleak-eyed stranger beside her. What was wrong with him? Why was he so angry? He was too big a man to be joining Cleo in a fit of the sulks over losing the game, so what was it? Instinctively, she knew that it was some crime that she, all unknowing, had committed—but what?

'Don't struggle—or I'll hurt you a damn sight more,' he said between his teeth, then, as she went to shy away, he gave her arm a savage squeeze and, ignoring her stifled cry, forced her out into the warm, silky water.

The two boys were at the far end of the beach, diving from the jetty where the boat was still moored which just yesterday, she realised with a jolt—it seemed more like a century ago—Alex had used to transport his unwilling captive. He stood frowning, with her pulled close in to his side, then, as one of the boys shouted to them, he gave an impatient exclamation and gestured to where the beach curved out into a line of low, dark rocks.

'Come out there.'

He released his grip and slipped out of his shorts, to reveal a pair of black, hip-hugging briefs, then plunged out into the water, making for the rocks with a rapid crawl. Selina stood for a moment, the water lapping round her knees, even now toying with the idea of defiantly heading back up the beach, but, quite unable to shake off the image of his dark, set face, she waded through the limpid green shallows and struck out towards the darker inky blue of the deeper water beyond.

The coolness closed deliciously around her hot body, but she was scarcely aware of it as she battled grimly to catch up with him. He did not stop until they were round the headland, out of sight of the beach, then he waited, treading water, until she came up to him.

'Right. Up here.'

He pulled himself on to a flat rock which shelved smoothly down into the sea, then turned back to her, holding out his hands, but she ignored them.

'I can manage, thank you.'

She hauled herself out and stood up slowly, uncomfortably aware as she did so of the nearness of his virtually naked body, of the waterdrops sparkling among the fuzz of fine dark hair on his chest, of the little rivulets coursing down his strong, hard-muscled thighs.

Abruptly, she removed her gaze and began instead to study intently the steep slope of hillside further along the coast, parched and barren above, changing to green terraces of vines and figs, and then a darker green as it reached the belt of pines and eucalyptus trees.

She was still furious with herself for so tamely obeying him, but she also grudgingly acknowledged that she had had no choice—she was just too wary of him in his present mood to dare to do otherwise. She plumped down on the rock and began industriously squeezing the fat plait of hair from which streams of water were trickling. But then suddenly her hands stilled.

'What did you say?' It came out as a gasp.

'I said,' Alex repeated grimly, 'that you appear to be in some danger of forgetting which Petrides brother you are married to.'

CHAPTER SIX

AT FIRST, Selina, her blue eyes darkening almost to the colour of Alex's own, could only gape at him in stupefaction, but then she snapped, 'Oh, don't be so ridiculous!'

His brows came down in an angry frown, but she continued to stare at him, then laughed in total incredulity. 'You—you're not *jealous* of Nik, are you?'

'When I see you kissing him like that—yes, I am. As I would be jealous of any man that you kissed. You are my wife,' he said savagely. 'You belong to me.'

'I don't belong to anyone,' she flared, all caution scattered to the winds. 'But, in case you're worried, I can assure you that there's no chance of my *ever* for one minute forgetting that I *belong* to you—even if you've done your best, for the last three years, to forget that *you* are married to me.'

'And just what do you mean by that, Selina *mou*?' His voice was icy cold.

'What I mean is, th-that,' she was stammering with righteous rage, 'every time I've picked up a glossy magazine, *you've* been in it with your l-latest—what do they call it?—oh, yes, *companion*, fawning all over you, and you——'

'Be quiet.' The fury just below the surface of his voice silenced her. 'The pictures—the gossip stories—don't you understand that all that was merely a charade, put on for your sake?'

'For *my* sake! Oh, yes, I'm——'

'Yes. To save you the humiliation of your pathetic story being splashed across the front pages of the gutter Press of Europe.'

'And I suppose you weren't worried about your own—humiliation?'

'Of course I was. What man would want the world to know that his bride of less than two hours has walked out on him?'

In spite of her still boiling anger, Selina felt a sudden disturbing twist of—what was it—guilt?—inside her breast, as he went on, 'Fortunately, the ceremony was in our private chapel, and everyone—priests, servants, the family, of course—was sworn to secrecy——' So she was right; a conspiracy of silence *had* been woven around her disappearance '—but if, overnight, Alex Petrides had stopped dating beautiful women,' his lips twisted in a cynical smile, 'then people would have begun asking questions. The scandalmongers, the *paparazzi*—well,' he shrugged, 'I had to keep them happy—and keep them away from you.'

As she gazed at him blankly, he went on impatiently, 'Would you—or your headmistress, I wonder—have enjoyed having that so-exclusive girls' school invaded by the rats of the gutter Press in search of Alexis Petrides' runaway child-bride? But it was, I promise you, all a charade.'

'Do you really expect me to believe that?' she

burst out. 'It looked to me as though you were enjoying every last minute of it. All those pictures at the Cannes Film Festival last year, with you and——'

She broke off abruptly as, in spite of herself, she remembered painfully how, during the last school holidays, she'd quite by chance stumbled across the photographs in an old magazine. She'd curled up on her bed, a tight ball of misery inside her, which had finally burst out in a torrent of tears. She'd gone down for dinner, very subdued and red-eyed, but fortunately her father had been so enraged by the two printing errors he'd discovered in yet another learned article of his that he'd not noticed a thing.

Somehow, she pulled herself together, but could only add lamely, 'Well, don't try to tell me that you weren't having a great time.'

'And what if I was? Just because you chose to shut yourself away in a nunnery for three years,' she winced at the acid in his voice, 'why should you object if I refused to lead a totally monastic existence?'

She knew she should have been quite uncaring, but for some obscure reason she *did* object—very violently. Alex must have seen her expression for his mouth tightened.

'No, *koukla mou*, it wasn't like that—not what you're thinking, I promise you.'

He picked up the hand which lay nearer to him and began smoothing his thumb across her soft palm. Backwards and forwards—there was something hypnotic about the sensuous, unhurried movement of his long, sensitive fingers. There was such beauty in those hands, such power . . .

Dimly, she heard him sigh. 'Oh, Selina. Why do you always bring out the worst in me?'

She looked up at him, and he smiled at her, the old Alex, just for a fleeting moment, and she thought, Oh, why does it have to be like this? Why did it all have to change so horribly? Their relationship had always been so good, so uncomplicated: a simple case of adoring, starry-eyed hero-worship on one side—she gave a tiny, rueful smile—and an affectionate, indulgent older second cousin on the other. If only it could have gone on like that forever . . .

Oh, wake up, she told herself bleakly. Of course it couldn't. Alex was her husband, now—and everything was different. Now, each time they came within speaking—or rather, snarling—distance of one another, the tension snaked around them, catching them both up in its coils. But couldn't they still be friends? That wasn't so impossible—surely?

She gave him a slightly tremulous smile.

'I'm sorry, Alex, if it seemed like that.' Then, as he raised his dark brows questioningly, 'With Nik, I mean. It's just, well, I'm very fond of him. He—he's such good fun. I suppose he's like the older brother I used to dream of having when I was a child. But you—you're so much more . . .'

Her voice tailed miserably away.

'Well, go on.' He gave her arm a little shake, and she bit her lip.

'S-so much more——' she had been about to say 'menacing', but broke off, seeking another, hopefully less provocative word, and finally came out with '—demanding.' But the hope was vain.

'*Demanding*?' It was almost a shout. 'Have I really been so demanding, Selina?' He seized her other arm, dragging her round to face him and she was terrified by the naked anger which she saw flaring in his eyes. 'Maybe I have not been demanding enough, but have allowed you to behave like the foolish, spoilt little girl you still are. Maybe I should have followed you to England and demanded that you return with me. Maybe, instead of treating you like a precious piece of porcelain, I should have forced myself on you—exacted my rights to your body by force. Is that what you would have preferred, Selina *mou*?'

His voice rang harshly in her ears, and she instinctively threw up her hands to free herself from his grip, but too late. Ignoring her wildly flailing arms, he pulled her to him. She tasted the salt on his lips, then his mouth was fierce against hers, his tongue forcing its way ruthlessly into her mouth. She gave a little wordless moan, begging to be released, but his only response was to strain her nearer to him, as though to fuse their two bodies into one.

One hand came up to drag down the strap of her bikini top, wrenching the wet, clinging material away in a brutal movement, then his splayed fingers had closed over her bare breast. His hand stilled for a moment, curving possessively to enjoy its ripe fullness, then, as those probing fingers brushed across its soft centre, she felt the flesh pucker into life, tauten and stand erect under his touch.

His mouth left hers and moved along the line of her chin, so that she arched her head, closing her eyes against the feel of his lips, burning hot against her skin. He fastened at last over her nipple, his mouth and teeth roughly sucking at it, until it almost seemed to strain towards him of its own volition.

She was lost in the turbulence of strange, terrifying emotions, the areola of her breast, all feeling centred on it, seemingly the very core of her being, until, as his impatient hands roved down her body, her sides, her belly, those feelings began coursing through every channel of her, creating newer, even more intense sensations.

But then she felt his fingers close on her bikini pants and in an instant she froze, a strangled sob bursting out of her. Panic-stricken, she clutched him, her fingers digging into his arms, her eyes wide and staring. Shuddering for breath, he drew back sharply and she saw the dusky flush along his tanned cheekbones. His eyes, black and brilliant, went to her swollen mouth, then his lips twisted and he pushed her from him so abruptly that, her head already reeling, she had to put her hands down hard against the rock to save herself from falling.

Next moment, he had leapt to his feet and dived headlong into the blue depths, his tanned body cleaving the water like an arrow. He surfaced yards away, tossed the water out of his black hair and, with not even a backward glance at her, he began swimming away, arm over arm, as though he were bent on reaching the North African coast.

She sat there for a long time, huddled on the rock and staring unseeingly until long after that retreating head had disappeared, then at last she roused, eased herself into the water and swam slowly back to the cove.

Alex did not reappear all day. In fact, it was not until she was dressing for dinner that she heard movements from his bedroom and then, from just the other side of that flimsy bathroom partition, the sound of the shower being switched on.

She stood, half in, half out of her white, cheesecloth dress, staring at the door, but when she heard the water cascading down she scrambled into it, fumblingly knotted the shoulder ties, and backed up against the far wall, waiting tensely for his inevitable arrival.

But then, a few minutes later, she heard his voice drifting up from the terrace, deep in conversation with his sister and her husband. Selina realised that she was standing as though rooted to the floor and she finally went across to the dressing-table, where she finished getting ready, pulling up her hair in a tight knot at the nape of her neck.

Even when the dinner gong went, though, she

lingered, and so most of the family were already at the table when she came through on to the terrace, feeling very self-conscious and keeping her eyes firmly away from the area where some instinct told her Alex was seated.

She kissed her grandmother and Thia Katrine, then, as she straightened, forced herself to raise her eyes to meet his. But he was not looking at her. Instead, he was bending over Poppi, who had perched herself on his lap, her plump hands full of some pretty shells which she was showing to him. The two dark heads, one large, one small, leaned close together in seemingly rapt attention, and Selina stared down at them, a strange tight feeling squeezing on her chest . . .

Someone—Sonia—was speaking to her, and she roused sufficiently to smile back and slip into the empty chair beside her, relieved to find that she was well screened from Alex.

Not that that had mattered, though, she thought miserably two hours later. Throughout the long ordeal of the meal, he hardly addressed a word to her, and whenever he looked at her, past the heads and shoulders in between them, it was barely a glance, their eyes just meeting then sliding past one another. Fortunately, everyone else was in a noisy, talkative, especially Greek sort of mood, so the fact that two of the family were eating their meal in virtual silence passed unnoticed.

When finally dinner ended, Selina longed to repeat her swift retreat of the previous evening, but pride—and the thought of Alex's reaction—forced her to join in the general exodus to the veranda at the front of the house, where coffee was being served. Alex, however, did not immediately follow them. Throwing him a swift, sidelong glance from under her lashes, she saw him get up from the table then disappear indoors with Sonia, carrying the sleepy Poppi in his arms.

Selina retreated to the far end of the veranda and sat down on an old wicker sofa. A maid handed her a cup of coffee and she cradled it in her lap, leaning her head against the cushioned back of the sofa and listening abstractedly to the general chatter, more subdued now, and the soothing clink of cups and glasses. Faintly, from the entrance hall, she could hear Alex's voice. It was a one-sided conversation—he must be on the telephone.

She half closed her eyes. Beyond the veranda it was bright moonlight, but here the rows of lamps on the wall above had been switched on and their soft yellow light filtered through the lacework pattern of vine leaves over her head. She felt herself drifting away.

'Would you like a liqueur?'

She was jolted abruptly out of her reverie to see Alex standing over her, the lights flickering through the leaves to make a moving shadow-play over his face, so that she could hardly make out his features.

'Oh, no, thank you.'

Deftly hooking across a small wicker table with his foot, he set down the coffee-cup and brandy balloon he was holding, then dropped down beside her. He sat back, his long legs sprawled out in front of him, apparently studying the toes of his navy canvas deck shoes, one arm thrown negligently along the back of the sofa.

As he moved slightly to reach for his glass, his fingers brushed against her bare shoulder. Selina, every sense suddenly alert, looked up just as Alex's head turned and, for the first time that evening, their eyes fully met. Next moment, with a slight grimace which only she was aware of, he withdrew his arm as though the contact with her bare flesh had burned him, and laid it instead on the no man's land of sofa between them.

Together, side by side, they smiled across at the others, joined in the groans at one of Nik's appalling medical-student anecdotes, but all the time Alex's presence was permeating her entire consciousness. What a perfect picture of a married couple they must be presenting. The bitter thought welled up in her, then, realising that she was gnawing viciously at her thumb-nail, she clenched both hands in her lap.

The awareness of him, his nearness, was growing inside her, so that she felt a suffocating sensation which was rapidly spiralling into acute claustrophobia. She glanced round furtively, just as he took a sip of brandy. He caught her eye, and something of her desperation must have communicated itself to him, for he asked quietly, his voice quite neutral,

'Are you all right?'

'Y-yes.' Her voice was so low that he had to bend

towards her to hear it. 'Do you think I could have some brandy, though?'

'I'll get you some,' he murmured.

'No.' She shrank from drawing attention to herself, certain that her face was pale with strain. 'If I could just have a sip of yours, please.'

He shrugged faintly then held his glass out to her and she took it, feeling the warmth from his fingers still linger on it, and smelling the potent fumes. She swallowed, letting the liquid fire run through her mouth and throat, setting them alight, until she almost choked, then she took a deep breath and determinedly downed several large gulps.

Firmly, he removed the glass from her hands, but those few hurried mouthfuls of neat golden fire had done the trick. They had subdued all that panic which had been fluttering wildly inside her, so that now she found the courage to get to her feet, murmur something about being rather tired still, and before Alex could move she had flashed everyone a dazzling, empty smile and was gone.

Upstairs, though, she could not settle; her mind was racing in overdrive. It must be that Greek coffee, so strong that you could almost stand a spoon in it. She pulled out her nightie from under her pillow, but then, instead of undressing, she sat down on the low window-sill, staring out. A full moon hung heavy in the blue-black sky, silvering the topmost branches of the olive trees and casting a pale sheen on the sea beyond, where—she could just hear it above the talking below—the waves shushed softly against the tiny pebbles which fringed the tide line.

Alex's voice rose and fell with the rest. He was obviously in no hurry to come upstairs—and yet, sooner or later, he *would* come. And when he did—she realised that she was clutching her hands together, the palms clammy in spite of the warmth of the summer night—when he came, surely he would continue what he had begun that morning? The fact that he had been casualness itself all evening only meant that he had recovered his poise, had got over that fit of anger which had temporarily saved her.

And yet that seeming casualness must have been a mask for the inner turmoil which he, as much as she, was feeling. After all, his pride, if nothing else, would make him want to ensure that not even the closest members of his—*their*—family realised just how fraught the situation was between them.

Down there, sitting by him on the sofa, she had felt suddenly as though the tension were stretching and stretching like a piece of steel wire already pulled to its furthest limit. Anything—a movement, a word—could at any moment rip it in two and send it lashing back in their faces.

Surely he would come to her tonight, determined to resolve matters with no further delay? And this time she would be quite unable to stop him. She ran the tip of her tongue around her lips, feeling the lower one still swollen from his savage onslaught.

She stared at the bathroom door, as though expecting at every moment to see it burst open, then, as somewhere in the house a floorboard

creaked, she sprang to her feet, fumbled open the
door, and was through into Alex's room, where the
moonlight lay in silver bars across his empty bed.

She ran along the passage and down the stairs on
the points of her toes, her lungs almost bursting
with pent-up tension. She was terrified that one of
the servants would be in the hall, but it was
deserted. They had obviously relaxed their guard
for the night, handing over sentry duty to the
family—or Alex.

From the open doorway, she could hear the
sound of conversation, louder than from her room,
but she was screened by the corner of the house.
There was a laugh, a chair scraped, then a shadow,
black and angular against the yellow lamplight,
as someone—Alex?—stood up and moved
towards her.

In three bounds, she had crossed the terrace and
was darting down through the moonlit garden. She
ran blindly, with no clear idea of where she was
running to, but somehow her feet carried her to the
olive grove, the old childish sanctuary.

The trees stood perfectly still, not the faintest
breath of wind stirring their grey branches, so that
they looked as though they had been moulded from
filigree silver. She wandered along the narrow
aisles, the wide hem of her white dress brushing
softly against the long grass, then finally sat down,
leaning against the rough trunk of one of the trees.
The absolute stillness, the peace of this place, acted
on her raw nerves like a soothing balm, until her
wildly thumping heart and erratic pulses slowed at

last . . .

'I somehow thought that I would find you here.'

She opened her eyes to see Alex looming over her and, as she stared wildly up at him, he went on, 'Don't you know that it's dangerous to sleep under an olive tree on a night of full moon? It will steal your soul away.'

He shot her a crooked little smile, but as he came down on his haunches beside her she saw that his eyes were very sombre.

'I—I couldn't sleep.' Her fingers were busy, pleating the already pleated cotton of her dress. 'It must be the coffee. I—I'm not used to it.'

'Of course.'

He eased himself down on to the ground, and she felt his hand close over hers. Somehow, she forced herself not to snatch it away, but he must have felt the tremors running through it for he began to stroke it, very gently, as though he were calming a captured wild animal. Then his fingers stilled. He glanced down, and, although his expression was quite unreadable, she knew that he was looking at the wide gold band of her wedding-ring.

'I had to find you,' he said softly. 'I couldn't let you go tonight without——' At the sight of her face, he broke off and gave a wry smile. 'You needn't have worried, *agape mou*. I was determined to leave you alone tonight. But I wanted to give you this.'

From his pocket, he took a small box and held it out to her. Wonderingly, she opened it and saw, nestling in a mound of white silk, a gold ring set with one large, single stone which glowed with milky luminescence in the moonlight. Her gaze went from the lovely object to Alex's inscrutable face.

'It's beautiful,' she murmured. 'What is it?'

'It's a moonstone.'

She took the ring from the box and held it up so that it gleamed with coldly translucent white fire. Without looking at him, she mumbled, 'It's—it's an engagement ring, isn't it?'

'Well, perhaps. The usual order, I believe,' his voice was dry, 'is for the giving of the engagement ring to precede the wedding. In our case, circumstances were rather exceptional, and now—well, you can regard it as you wish. But I bought it for you, and no other woman will ever have it.'

'Oh.'

Unable still to meet his eyes, she was slipping the ring back into the box when he said, 'Wear it for me, Selina, at least——'

He broke off, but, moved by an indefinable something in his voice, she gave it to him then obediently held out her left hand. He stood up, raising her with him, then, as he slid the ring on to her finger, he said,

'A moonstone seemed somehow fitting. The stone of the moon for the goddess of the moon. Selina, the huntress, the moon goddess.' Again that small, crooked smile. 'Your parents chose more wisely than they knew when they named you for her. They must have foreseen that remote, ethereal quality in you. And tonight, above all . . .'

His eyes moved over the white dress, gleaming soft silver, like her skin, then very slowly he leaned towards her and she felt his warm breath on her cheek. The moonlight was doing strange things to her senses, making her pulses quicken erratically once more. Alex was going to kiss her and this time she was not going to resist.

She half closed her eyes to receive his kiss, but all he did was gently release her hair and let it fall to her shoulders, allowing it to drift through his fingers like strands of pale silk.

She heard his breath catch softly in his throat. 'How beautiful you are. But, *agape mou*——' he shot her the ghost of a rueful smile '——you still remind me of a young girl on one of the friezes in the Acropolis Museum. She stands poised, turned to face the darkness—the unknown—ahead of her, but she has one hand raised and her head is turned back as though in fear of leaving the security of the light. And so she remains, trapped in the marble, frozen forever between the two.'

Lifting his hand, he traced the outline of her soft mouth, and almost imperceptibly she felt herself begin to sway towards him——

Heavy footsteps were blundering towards them and they jerked apart. The two boys, clutching towels, burst through the trees a few yards away, veered off when they saw them and went racing on towards the beach.

They stood motionless until the sounds had died away, then Alex took her hands and, raising them to his lips, kissed them. She stared down at his bent head, strange, unnerving emotions warring within her.

'Alex . . .' she whispered huskily, but he had already taken a step back, away from her

'Go back to the villa. *Now.*' When she did not move, 'I'll stay here a little longer——like you, I don't think I shall sleep tonight.' He gave her the briefest of smiles. 'You're right——it must be that coffee. But don't worry, I shan't disturb you.' And he turned away.

The gesture was an abrupt dismissal, but Selina, her hands still prickling from the touch of his warm lips, stood watching him. But then at last she walked slowly back towards the villa, her mind in a whirling turbulence which blotted out all rational thought. She glanced back just once, and saw him leaning against the same tree. His arms were folded and he was staring at the ground.

CHAPTER SEVEN

SELINA opened her eyes to daylight, her first conscious thought that, against all the odds, she had slept. Almost as soon as she had returned to her room and undressed, in fact, she must have plunged headlong into a deep, black well of sleep.

She lay for some minutes, straining to catch any sign of movement from Alex, but no sounds came so she swiftly showered and dressed. She hesitantly opened the door to his room and peeped in, expecting to see his dark head on the pillow, but his bed was empty. The sheet was rumpled, though. So he had come back here then, and not, as she'd half feared, spent the whole night in the olive grove. He'd probably gone down to the pool for a pre-breakfast swim. Maybe she would join him—a first tentative step, perhaps, towards getting their relationship into a slightly less fraught state.

But Alex was not in the pool. He was seated, on his own, at the breakfast table, and when he saw her he gave her a brief impersonal smile, a polite '*Kalimera*, Selina,' and then immediately switched his attention back to the sheaf of papers he had been flipping through.

She slid into the chair opposite, poured herself some coffee, then sat covertly watching him over the rim of her cup, seeing his dark blue eyes, half hidden by the heavy fringe of stubby black lashes, as he skim-read each sheet in turn, occasionally pausing to frown slightly. There were fine lines at the outer corners of his eyes, white against the tanned skin, and there was a tautness about his mouth . . . She stared at each of his familiar features in turn, lingering on them, until suddenly, as though feeling her intent gaze on him, he looked up. Their eyes met, then abruptly he swilled down the last remnants of coffee, pushed back his chair and stood up.

'I have to go to Athens this morning.'

'Oh.'

She set down her cup, jarring it against the saucer, and registered for the first time that he was wearing, not casual beach clothes, but a white shirt, very formal in cut although the top two buttons were undone, and a pair of lightweight silver-grey trousers.

'I—I didn't know.'

'Yes, well, something urgent has cropped up—something which I am needed for.'

'But how long will you be away?' she blurted out.

He shrugged carelessly. 'A couple of days perhaps.' He picked up the pile of papers, briskly shuffled them into order, then came round to her side of the table and stood looking down at her. 'You are still very pale, *koukla*. Enjoy yourself while I am away—remember, you are on holiday.'

She glanced up at him quickly, but there did not seem to be the slightest irony behind his words. And then he was gone—without a kiss, a goodbye, a backward look—almost as if he was actually *glad* to go, she thought, with a needling little burst of resentment.

She sat listening to his retreating footsteps, then reached for a soft bread roll and began carefully spreading it with the pale Greek butter, but then, on a sudden impulse, she thrust the plate away and jumped to her feet.

She found him in the large room at the back of the villa which, with its battery of computer terminals, fax machine and teleprinter, served as the summer centre of the fingers-in-every-pie Petrides' business empire. He was standing at the desk, his back to her, putting manila folders into a slimline black document case.

Selina stood staring at him, watching those busy hands. Then, although she had made no sound, he must have become aware of her standing behind him, and he swung round. Just for a moment, there seemed to be—*something* in his eyes, but it was gone so swiftly that she knew she'd imagined it.

'Yes?' The formal politeness chilled her to the bone, and when she did not—could not—reply, he added impatiently, 'You wanted something, Selina?'

All of a sudden, she knew what she wanted. She wanted him to ask her to go with him to Athens. Of course, she wouldn't—that just would not be sensible. But all the same . . .

'Alex,' she began, but then, as she took a small step towards him, footsteps came rapidly down the passage behind her.

'Morning, Selina. My, you're up early—coming to see him off?'

Nik's dark hair was tousled and he was still jamming his T-shirt into the waistband of his shorts. He grinned at her as he came past, but then, as he looked swiftly from one to the other of them, added, 'I'll come back if you like, Alex——'

'No.' His brother's voice was clipped. 'I'm quite ready.' He glanced at Selina. 'Nik is running me into Tinos Town to get the morning ferry across to Mykonos for the Athens plane. There is no need for you to come with us.'

Without waiting for a reply, he turned away and snatched a sheet of paper from the maw of one of the chattering machines, and glanced briefly at it before crumpling it into the waste-paper basket. Then he put on a pale grey jacket which was slung across the desk, quickly rolled up the blue silk tie beside it, thrust it into his pocket and picked up his briefcase.

She stood back to let them pass, automatically answering both men's goodbyes and watching them go off down the passage, their tall figures framed against the sunlight from the open door, then she went slowly back to the terrace.

A maid had brought out a fresh pot of coffee. As she poured herself a cup, she heard a car roar into life then swing away behind the villa and up the winding drive which led through the cypresses to the Tinos road.

The first long day passed, then the second, sliding

into the third. The crisis, whatever it was, was clearly taking time to resolve—either that, or Alex was in no hurry to return. Either way, she couldn't bring herself to ask any of the family—not even Nik—if they had any idea when he was coming back.

She spent hours lounging by the pool and sunbathing on the beach, her delicate skin carefully protected so that, instead of turning shrimp-pink, as she usually did, she was developing a thoroughly becoming light golden tan. She could have been lonely—with Alex's abrupt departure, Cleo had become even more moody, and Nik, having apparently registered that the resit of the pathology exam he'd failed dismally in June was now just over the horizon, had shut himself away, surrounded by piles of formidable-looking medical text books. But there was Poppi—the little girl seemed to have taken a great fancy to her. Selina had begun giving her swimming lessons in the pool each morning, and her uncomplicated company and lisping Greek were somehow very soothing to her jagged nerves.

All the same, though, while everyone else dozed in the heat of the afternoon, she would find herself wandering aimlessly around the villa and grounds, until, each day, her meandering footsteps finally led her to Alex's room. She would smooth the already smooth cotton cover, carefully straighten each of the Greek rugs, pick up and set down the things on his dressing-table: brushes and combs, a set of keys, and a photograph of his mother and father.

One afternoon, as she sat on the dressing-table stool she found her hand straying towards the top drawer. She hesitated, then slid it open. Handkerchiefs, a couple of silk cravats, and—— She stared down, peculiar feelings twisting at her inside, then slowly lifted out the photograph in its frame. She remembered so clearly when it had been taken—just a couple of days after she'd arrived on that climactic second occasion, when Alex was still, for a short while longer, only her second cousin.

Who had taken it? She frowned, as though it had become important to remember. Yes, that was right—Sonia. She and Nik were sitting side by side at the edge of the pool, their legs dangling in the blue water. He was smiling round at her, but she—she was looking past his shoulder at someone who wasn't on the photograph. Alex had just that moment appeared, in swimming-trunks, a towel slung over his arm, and she was staring across at him, her lips parted, a strange, intent expression on her face, a yearning—almost a hunger. But that was impossible—quite impossible . . .

She stared down at it a moment longer, then suddenly slammed it back into the drawer and got up. The wardrobe door had swung open slightly; she went to close it, but then, instead, found herself opening it wider. She stood, for several minutes perhaps, letting her hand trail across his shirts, trousers, casual jackets, still imbued with the faintest sandalwood aroma from his body.

There were no winter clothes here, and only beach shoes and espadrilles below. The villa was for the summer, and by the time the brief Greek winter came, with its sudden storms lashing the grey sea, he would be back in Athens again ... And she—where would she be? She closed the wardrobe door, went through to her room and lay down on the bed, in a vain attempt to sleep the afternoon away.

On the fifth morning, after Selina had given Poppi her swimming lesson, Nik asked her to help him with his revision, and together they slogged through pages of pathology—the Greek making it even more unintelligible to her—until her head was reeling. Suddenly, he snatched up the book impatiently and hurled it across the lawn.

'That's it. I can't stand any more. Come on—let's go into town.'

When they arrived—or rather, when they scorched into Tinos in Nik's scarlet MG—they wandered for a while among the narrow, bustling streets, looking in through the open fronts of the bazaar-like shops, their embroidered rugs, woollen sweaters, leather bags, beaten copperware, all temptingly spilling out on the pavements.

'Do you want anything?' Nik asked.

'No—not today, anyway, thanks.'

And yet there was something she knew she had to do—something which could not be put off any longer. Nik had sauntered on down the street, leaving her by a small shop selling souvenirs. She darted inside, bought two postage stamps, snatched two identical postcards from a rack, and wrote two identical messages: 'I have had a change of plans. I am with Alex on Tinos.'

She stared down at the bald words, knowing that she ought to write more but quite unable to, then addressed them to her father and Aunt Grace. As she stood with the cards already half in the box, she thought, Once posted, they will take on a momentum of their own, leading to—what? But then, as Nik came up to her, she thrust them in.

'How about a drink? I could do with one.' He steered her through the congested streets, until they reached a pavement café alongside the harbour. 'What a crowd! The build-up to the *Paniytrie* gets earlier each year.'

'The *Paniytrie*?' Selina queried.

'Yes, you know, the pilgrimage to the ikon of the Virgin.'

Of course. She remembered now being told on her previous visits of how, every fifteenth of August, half the inhabitants of Greece, or so it seemed, squeezed themselves on to Tinos to celebrate the miraculous appearance of the gorgeous, jewel-encrusted ikon which she had gazed at, spellbound, when on her first visit her grandmother had taken her to the white marble church of Panagia Evangelistria.

'We took off last year,' Nik went on. 'It was just too crowded—standing room only across the whole island—so we went across to your grandmother's island for a few days. It's quite primitive, of course, but we're planning on going again this year—in the next day or so, in fact.' He paused to take a long drink of his ice-cold lager, then went on, his voice quite bland, 'So Alex should be back by then.'

'Oh, yes, I—I expect so.'

She was looking down at her chilled orange, her fingers circling the rim of her glass, when she heard him say, 'We're all so pleased you're back with us, Selina. You know that, don't you?'

She glanced up in sudden confusion to see that his eyes, usually sparkling with humour, were regarding her very seriously. She looked away across the wide bay towards where the motley array of white-hulled boats were swinging easily at anchor.

'Yes, of course,' she said at last, but then heard herself add, 'Well, *nearly* all of you, anyway.'

'Cousin Cleo, you mean?' When she nodded reluctantly, he went on, 'Yes, well, as you saw the other day, she never was a good loser.'

Selina hesitated, but she had to know. 'You mean—Alex?'

Nik did not reply at once, but looked at her, lips pursed, as though he were making some clinical decision. Then, 'She's been crazy about Alex for years—and her parents were all for it.'

'All for it?' she repeated stupidly.

'For them to marry. It was, oh, five or six years ago now. There was a terrible row, of course—a real Petrides blockbuster.' He smiled reminiscently, but then, as he caught sight of her expression, went on quickly, 'But Alex had got her measure long before then, and anyway,' his large brown hand closed over hers comfortingly, 'he married you, didn't he?'

'But that was only because my mother and grandmother wanted——' She broke off.

'Wanted him to marry you, you mean? Yes, of course they did. But, my sweet Selina,' he rolled his eyes expressively, 'don't you know my brother well enough yet to realise that the person has not been born who could make Alex Petrides do anything—*anything*—that he did not wish to do? Unless, of course,' he flashed her a wicked, slanting grin, 'that person's you.'

Before she could react, he had got to his feet and was fishing some coins from his jeans pocket.

'Duty calls, I'm afraid. Back to the pathology.'

'Come on, Poppi, nearly there.'

Selina stretched out her arms and, as the little girl floundered through the water, she caught her wrists and towed Poppi gently to her.

'I did it, didn't I, S'lina?'

'You did, my pet. Well done.'

Catching Poppi up in her arms, she dropped a kiss on her snub nose, and the child put her arms round her neck and hugged her.

'One more time, S'lina.'

'No.' She shook her head firmly. 'You're tired.' But then she added, as the girl's face fell, 'We'll have another go this afternoon.'

Poppi smiled up at her, then, looking past her, cried, quite without any warning, 'Oh, Thios

Alex—Thios Alex!'

Selina swung round. He had been leaning against the base of the diving platform, at the far end of the pool, but now he straightened up and came towards them. He had obviously just got back—he was still wearing the sleek grey trousers, the jacket slung from one shoulder—and, as she watched him approach, she was taken completely unawares by the wave of intense joy which swept through her whole body, so that she had to cling for a moment to the pool rail.

'Thios Alex, S'lina's teaching me to swim. Look.'

Poppi paddled frantically over to him, and he dropped his jacket on to a sun-lounger then squatted on his haunches at the edge of the pool.

'Very good, *koukla*. Keep it up, and you'll be in the next Olympics squad.' He leaned forward and, ignoring her protests, lifted her out. 'Didn't I hear Selina say that you were tired?'

He enfolded the child in a pink beach towel and, with a last cherubic smile at them both, she trotted off towards the villa.

The last remnants of joy had receded. Selina hauled herself awkwardly out of the water and, when he did not move, walked slowly over to him.

'H-hello, Alex.' She half lifted her hand, but then, as he made no response, she let it fall again. There was no warmth, no gladness to be back—*nothing* in those aloof navy eyes. 'Did——' Something was sticking in her throat. She cleared it away and tried again. 'Did you have a good trip?'

This time, the words came out huskily low.

'Yes, thank you.' But his voice was non-committal. 'I achieved what I went to do.'

'Oh, well, good,' she said lamely, then, not quite sure what he meant and quite unable to meet his eye any longer, she let her gaze flicker down to where her toe was slowly tracing the embossed pattern in the turquoise tiles.

'I came to tell you to get ready. We're leaving.'

'Leaving?' The word came out shrill. What did he mean? Had he—her heart leapt for an instant—had he tired of the game, admitted defeat, and was he letting her go? But no—he'd said *we're* leaving, hadn't he? She realised that he was still speaking.

'We're going across to your grandmother's island for a few days.'

Light dawned. 'Oh, you mean for the *Paniytrie*.'

A strange feeling was seeping through her. The disappointment, the frustration that, after her wild hope of a moment before, he wasn't releasing her after all, was being submerged in another emotion that she couldn't identify.

To cover her uncertainty, she babbled on, 'Nik told me you were planning to go there. But I didn't know that Grandmother owned a whole island.'

He smiled briefly. 'It's a very small island, as you'll see—too small to be even a speck on most maps. But you'll like it, I think.' He regarded her, his eyes sombre, then, 'So, if you will go and get a few things together—straight away.'

There was the slightest undercurrent of tension

in his final words. She glanced at him and saw the lines beside his mouth, surely even tauter than before. This business trip had obviously left him tetchy and irritable—and now he was clearly anxious to be off as soon as possible.

Quickly slipping on her wrap, she said, 'Well, I'll go then.'

She paused, half expecting him to come with her, but he merely said briskly, 'That's right, I'll see you later,' and, picking up his discarded jacket, he turned away, leaving her to gather up her sunglasses, sun-lotion and book, and drop them into her beach bag.

Back in the villa, no one seemed to be around. Thrown into confusion, no doubt, by Alex's lightning decision to leave for the island right now, without even waiting for lunch, everyone must be in their bedrooms feverishly packing.

She dragged off her wet bikini, showered, then slipped into her pink cotton shorts and white halter-neck blouse. Hastily, she pulled a comb through her wet hair, securing it into a pony-tail with a pink towelling band. Tugging open her wardrobe, she fished out a couple of cotton blouses and skirts, her denim shorts and a T-shirt. She hesitated. That was enough—they would presumably be away for only two or three days. On the other hand, though, she could imagine Cleo, at this very moment, filling a dozen suitcases with sufficient glamorous outfits to last her a month in Athens . . .

So, maybe something for the evening. She took

out the simple white sun-dress with the shoulder ties, then reached out from the back of the wardrobe a dress which a friend in Oxford had insisted on lending her, and which was far more sophisticated than anything she normally wore: black cotton jersey, with a slightly flared skirt, softly draped, demure bodice—and a sinfully plunging back.

She paused, her hand on the hanger, then snatched it out, threw it on top of the white dress, and bundled her dripping bikini into a plastic bag, squeezing that in on top along with her toilet bag.

As she was breathlessly zipping up her case, she heard from below raised voices. Oh, no, not more exuberant Greek high spirits, she thought, with a faintly wry smile, but then, Surely it sounds more like a blazing row?

She crossed to the open window and leaned out, but no one was in sight. She could hear Nik, though, expostulating loudly—it was too rapid for her to follow the words—Alex's more measured tones, then Nik again, this time slightly more equable.

But then Cleo's voice intervened, in shrill protest—a protest presumably aimed at Alex, for, after a long diatribe, Selina heard his voice break in with a curt authority which silenced the girl instantly. A few seconds later a door slammed, making every shutter in the house rattle.

Selina was still by the window when she heard Alex next door. She counted up to a hundred, then knocked.

'Peraste.'

He had already changed into denim shorts and a navy vest. A case stood open on the bed and he was tossing in a pair of jeans.

'Yes?'

'I'm ready.'

'Good.' But he scarcely glanced at her.

'I was wondering—can I help you pack?'

His smile was faintly ironic.

'If you wish, Selina.' He gestured to where his grey suit lay slung across a chair. 'You can put that away—and this.' Picking up a cream silk suit from the bed, he threw it across to her, then turned away to continue cramming clothes into his case.

She hung up the grey suit, then slid the cream one on to its padded hanger. She brushed it down with her hand, smoothing out a crease from the fine tusser silk. How handsome he must look wearing this—but she would never see him in it . . . If she was a proper wife, she could do this for him every time he went away on business . . . Meeting his eyes in the mirror, she suddenly became very busy hanging up the suit to try to hide the blush which had flared carnation-pink in her cheeks.

Back in her own room, she was picking up her case when she caught sight of the small box on the dressing-table, where it had stood untouched since that night in the olive grove. She stared at it for a long moment, then unzipped her case again and jammed it in.

Alex was waiting on the terrace, his fingers drumming an impatient tattoo on the wooden stair-rail.

'Right, let's go.' He took her case from her. 'I've said goodbye to your grandmother and Thia Katrine for you.'

She stared at him. 'Why? Aren't they coming?'

'No, they're not,' he said briefly. 'Now, come on.'

It was not until he slowed at the jetty that she finally managed to catch up with him. Beads of sweat were gathering over her upper lip and she wiped the back of her hand across her mouth. She shot him a baleful look.

'You're in a hurry, aren't you?'

But, instead of replying, he continued down the jetty and tossed their two cases into the well of the boat. He turned back to her, but she stood motionless, ignoring his outstretched hand. Something had been plucking at her mind all through the hectic flight through the olive grove, and now she looked round in bewilderment.

'Where are the others?'

The villa had been wrapped in silence when they left, so—her blue eyes flew to Alex.

'That's right. We're going alone.'

CHAPTER EIGHT

'GOING alone?' Selina could only idiotically echo Alex's words, as the panic flared wildly in her. 'I—we most certainly are not!'

Then, as he still held his hand out to her, his lips tightening angrily, she retreated a few steps and thrust her hands behind her back. Since his return, Alex had seemed—different. Not safe, exactly—a man like Alex was never safe, she thought grimly—even more irritable and impatient, yes, but somehow, in a strange, intangible way, less menacing. Now, though, the spectre of what would happen once they were totally alone and she helpless to save herself reared itself up like a sea-monster from the lower depths of her mind.

'I won't go,' she repeated defiantly, but then, terrified by the fury igniting in his eyes, she turned to run.

Alex caught her in two strides, swinging her round so that she fetched up against his chest, her free hand splayed against the hard muscles and sinew.

'You are coming, Selina,' he said tightly, 'if only because, on this occasion at least, I am not going to allow you to make a fool of me.'

Steering her in front of him, her knees buckling under her, he forced her down into the boat. As she collapsed on to the narrow seat, Alex untied the

ropes, leapt down beside her and the next moment
the powerful engine had burst into life. He reversed
the boat, far too fast, almost scraping the jetty
supports, then, opening the throttle to full, turned
for the open sea.

The island really was tiny. They were upon it
almost before she saw it and now, from close in,
everything seemed to be in miniature: a small bay,
bounded by two low, rocky headlands, and a
minuscule half-circle of creamy sand backed by
steeply rising slopes that climbed to a single
pine-fringed summit.

Alex cut the engine and floated the boat in to lie
alongside the nailed planks which served as a
rough landing-stage. He had not even glanced at
her the whole journey, keeping all his attention on
the sea ahead, and something in the angry hunch
of his shoulders, the determined jut of his hard jaw,
sent butterflies of apprehension flittering around
her stomach. But this time, she vowed fiercely to
herself, her fear was going to be kept firmly out of
sight.

He turned suddenly, catching the tail-end of the
scowl she had been safely directing at his
shoulder-blades, and his black brows came down
in an answering scowl. He came down the boat and
stood over her, regarding her very much as though
she were some slimy creature that had just crawled
out from its den in the waterlogged planking.

'How is it,' he said at last, 'that you unfailingly
bring out the worst in me, even when I am

trying—very hard?'

'Oh, are you? I hadn't noticed.' She quailed inwardly at his expression, but then, remembering her new iron resolution to defy him at all costs, added pertly, 'Maybe it's because there's so much of the worst in you.'

She saw his hands, just level with her eyes, bunch into fists momentarily, then he rammed them into his shorts pockets.

'Be very careful, Selina *mou*. I have already taken far more from you than from anyone else who has ever crossed my path. You are an extremely provoking child, and my fingers itch to put you over my knee and administer the salutary correction you richly deserve.' He took a deep breath. 'However, I will not allow you to provoke me—at least, not at present. Now, come.'

Set among the pines was a small, whitewashed house in a neat garden. They walked down a narrow path, one side edged with tomato plants, the other with tall sunflowers. As Alex put down the cases among the pots of geraniums on the porch, a plump, elderly woman in a black dress appeared in the open doorway.

At the sight of them, she clutched her hands together, giving little birdlike cries of joy, then, while Selina looked on in silent astonishment, she seized on Alex, hugging his tall figure to her ample bosom and letting fly with a hail of staccato Greek which Selina gave up on after the first couple of words.

At last, he disengaged himself, kissed her on both cheeks, then, before Selina could move out of range, he put his arm possessively round her waist, firmly drawing her forward.

'Selina, this is Lefkia. She was my nurse. No,' he frowned, searching for the exact English word, 'my nanny, when I was a child.'

Next moment, the woman had fastened on Selina, pulling her too into a close embrace. Selina stiffened, holding back slightly—she had, after all, been brought up never to show strong emotion, particularly affection. But being enclosed in those loving arms was rather like tumbling, when very cold and weary, into a warm, soothing bath, and she found herself putting her arms around the stout waist and hugging her back.

At last, Lefkia drew back, looked searchingly into her face, then, as though satisfied with what she saw there, nodded and said something incomprehensible to Alex. He smiled briefly, then turned to Selina.

'Lefkia informs me that Kyria Petrides is a very beautiful young lady.'

As Selina smiled at the woman uncertainly, she held her at arm's length, ran a disconcerting eye down her body, then patted the curve of her hips and flat stomach with obvious approval, laughed and said something more to Alex.

He smiled once more, but Selina, ever watchful where he was concerned, saw that yet again the smile did not remotely touch his eyes, and this time he did not translate.

Lefkia gestured them to two old chairs and disappeared back into the house. They sat, Selina in constrained silence, Alex staring moodily at the nearest sunflower, until she bustled out with a tray on which were two small cups of black coffee, two glasses of water and a dish of pink Turkish delight. Selina loathed the gooey sweetmeat and opened her mouth to make a polite refusal, but Alex's foot gave hers a warning nudge, so she smiled her thanks and somehow managed to force down a chunk while he set about the rest with every appearance of intense enjoyment.

There were more hugs and kisses, then he picked up the cases and they set off along a narrow stone path which skirted the pines.

'I had to take you there first,' Alex remarked. 'Lefkia would never have forgiven me if I had not immediately presented my young bride for her inspection.'

She glanced sharply up at him, her lips tightening at the sardonic expression on his face. Then, when he added carelessly, 'I hope you didn't mind?' she retorted,

'Would it have mattered if I had?'

'Not really. While you are with me, you will show good manners, and particularly to those who are of lower rank than yourself.'

The chill reproof stung her. Two bright red spots of colour appeared high on her cheekbones, but she bit her lip against the angry response and forced herself to take two long, calming breaths. If she allowed a raging row to develop between them, she

knew very well who would come out on top—and
it wouldn't be her . . . As never in her life before,
she needed to keep her cool now. True, they weren't
absolutely alone on this horrible island, as she'd
feared, but Lefkia, Alex's adoring slave, was
hardly likely to intervene if—oh, come on, who
was she fooling?—*when* he chose to take full
possession of her. After all, she was just another
Petrides property, wasn't she?

'I've always been very attached to her.' His tone
was milder, as if he too was prepared to draw back
from the brink—for the time being, at least. 'When
Yannis, her husband, was injured in an accident and
lost his job, I offered them the house here, where
they could take care of the island for us.'

Selina's eyes roamed over the hillside, the slopes
silver with eucalyptus, everywhere the creeping
wild thyme filling the air with its sharp perfume,
and below them, beyond the pines, a wide crescent
of dark blue sea, with Tinos an insubstantial blur
in the misty heat haze.

'I expect you get a lot of people trying to land
here.'

He laughed shortly. 'Actually, not too many.
Maybe it's something to do with Yannis's
twelve-bore shotgun, which he's never separated
from, and his pair of ravening mastiffs.'

She silently digested this, then went on, 'I didn't
know you'd had a nanny.'

'Oh, yes,' he said drily. 'My mother never had
much time for us when we were children. Perhaps
Sonia a little—she was, after all, a girl and could

be played with, dressed up like a doll. But Nik and I——' she saw him grimace as though he had touched an old wound '—were, I think, too like our father.'

'Oh, Alex, I'm sorry.'

Intensely moved by the aching bruise in his voice, she instinctively put out her hand, but then, as she felt his arm stiffen, she just as quickly dropped it to her side again.

The house, when they reached it, was very simple—long and low, its walls fading cream stucco, and shaded by tall cypress trees. There was no real garden, but the rough lawn was bordered by almond trees, two or three orange trees, the fruit already glowing ripe among the dark green leaves, and a huge spreading mulberry.

But the utterly simple lines of the house and its surroundings were, she realised, as she stood on the wooden veranda, the most perfect foil in the world for what lay beyond the tops of the pines—seemingly the whole of the southern Mediterranean stretching away to a silver infinity. She stood motionless, feeling her breath catch in her throat at the serene beauty of this place . . .

Suddenly conscious of Alex's eyes on her, she quickly wiped the rapture from her face.

'Would you like something to eat?' His voice was clipped.

'Oh, no, thank you. But is there a cold drink?'

'Of course—all modern amenities,' he added drily, 'including a refrigerator run on an electric generator. Wait here.'

He gestured her towards a wooden rocking-chair and went on into the house. Along the edge of the veranda was a row of old woody lavender bushes. She put a hand through the rails, broke off a spike, and leaned back, crushing the purple flower head between her fingers to release the pungent oil, and sniffed at it, concentrating all her being into that aroma, the glorious view, the rustle of the pines in the hot breeze, and blanking off that corner of her mind where the insidious fears still writhed and twisted.

'Iced lime juice—OK?'

'Mmm, lovely.'

Alex set down a jug, its sides frosting in the hot air, poured a glass for each of them, then handed her one.

'No Turkish delight, I'm afraid.'

Unexpectedly, he grinned at her, and before she could prevent it she found herself smiling back, but then just as quickly she looked away and took a long gulp at the drink. As she was putting down the glass, she remembered something.

'What did she—Lefkia say to you just before we left?'

For a split second, he hesitated, then, without looking at her, 'She was giving you the once-over, professionally speaking. She informed me that, with those hips, you will bear me many fine healthy sons.'

'Oh.'

The lime juice had spilled all over her hand. She dug out a handkerchief from her shorts pocket and scrubbed it clean, while the colour hammered in her cheeks.

'You must excuse her.' His voice was quite unemotional. 'I imagine that as she's been concerned with babies all her life they are still her main preoccupation.' He paused and she felt his gaze on her. 'But in any case, *koukla mou*, you need have no fear. That is not going to arise.'

'W-why not?'

'Because I am releasing you.'

'Releasing me?' She stared at him, wide-eyed, but he was looking out to sea at a tiny fishing caique on the far horizon.

'Yes—letting you go. Back to your home, to England—where you can begin divorce proceedings.'

'Oh.' She was totally incapable of any further response.

'That is what you want, is it not, Selina?'

'Well, yes, of course,' she stammered, still barely capable of speech.

'After all,' just for a moment the flat calm of his voice was disturbed by a flaying bitterness which made her wince, 'there has been no change in your—situation. Your grounds for annulment remain—like you—intact. While I was in Athens, I consulted our family lawyer.'

She gaped at him—so things had already been set moving. So fast—so soon. Alex must have misread her expression, for he said quickly, 'There is no need for you to worry. Theodore is very discreet. Some of the story is bound to come out—that is unavoidable—but we shall protect you as much as we can from the publicity.'

'But—but I don't understand.' Her mind had almost ceased to function.

'It's quite simple, Selina *mou*.' He gave her a rueful smile. 'Put me down as an arrogant Greek male, if you like, but I really believed that all I had to do was get you back out here and you would fall into my arms with cries of gratitude. But then, once you were here again, you very soon proved me wrong and I have come to realise that you were right and it was indeed all a dreadful mistake.'

He paused and turned his head to look at her, the faintest glimmer in his eyes.

'Well—try and look more pleased. After all, I am giving you what you want, am I not?'

'What?' She spoke abstractedly, her mind still grappling with his words, but then she said fervently, 'Oh, yes, of course.' And yet, why wasn't she more relieved—in fact, over the moon at his decision? She wasn't—not in the least . . . But she thrust these disturbing thoughts from her.

'That is why I went to Athens. I needed to think, away from the family—and you. I had already made up my mind that there would be no repeat of that morning, out on the rock, when I almost took you by force.' His voice was harsh with self-disgust. 'I had waited three years for you, but I swore to myself that I would never possess you unless you came to me of your own free will. I could, even now, have your body, but that way I would never have your spirit, your mind, your soul.

And so, Selina *mou*,' that odd little smile again, 'I am setting you free.'

Setting her free? He was really prepared, for her sake, to do that? She stared at him, wonderingly, but then, out of the fog which was shrouding her brain, leapt one coherent thought.

'The dowry,' she blurted out. 'What about that?'

He muttered something under his breath. 'I have already told you the dowry is of no account. I bitterly regret having told you about it—I was, of course, merely trying to put more pressure on you. But you will put it out of your mind forever. You will not speak of it again.'

'All right, I won't.' But, whether he agreed or not, somehow she would repay him. Then another thought struck her. 'If you're letting me go, why have you brought me here?'

He spread his hands expressively. 'We Greeks have a reputation for being hospitable to—foreigners.'

Was he including her among the 'foreigners'? The faint underlining of the word made her sure that he was, and a feeling, not exactly of sadness, but of regret, seeped momentarily into her mind. He was shutting her out from Greece, from the family, and from himself

'You came here for a holiday. Very well, I can ensure that you have one. But it was necessary to withdraw you from the others. Dearly though I love them, they are——' he pulled a face '—always present. They all know our history, and therefore despite my orders, the pressures on you are always there. And therefore, Selina,' he stood up, lifting her to her feet, 'you need have no fear. For a few days, I shall be once more the second cousin that I think you still yearn for—and nothing more.'

CHAPTER NINE

SHEER gratitude was surging through Selina, mingling with the astonishment and relief so that she could not speak. But, in any case, Alex did not seem to want a response.

He had turned to pick up the two cases and was leading the way indoors, through a sitting-room, all pale, sea-washed colours and simply furnished with cane armchairs and sofas, then into a cool, dark passage which ran the whole length of the house.

'Lefkia said she has prepared everything for us,' he remarked as he pushed open the nearest door with his elbow.

He walked in and threw open a shutter, then stopped dead, turning to her with that curious grimace, almost of distaste, which she was coming to know so well.

'This is normally my room. I had forgotten that Lefkia, of course, assumed that we should be sharing it.' He shot her a wry smile. 'When I am alone, she does not usually go in for such floral pyrotechnics, but I suppose it was her way of welcoming my new wife.'

Selina, looking around the room, saw that on every halfway level surface there were vases and jugs, all of them crammed with flowers—huge spikes of gladioli, whole sheaves of carnations and bowls of long-stemmed white and yellow daisies.

'Oh, that's so kind of her!' she exclaimed. 'It must have taken her hours.'

But then, as she stared down at a cracked kitchen cup on the bedside table, overflowing with nasturtiums and sprigs of silver lavender, they all at once blurred and danced in front of her eyes, and she turned away.

Alex lifted her case on to the bed. 'You will have this room. I think you will find it the coolest.' He walked across to one corner and opened a door. 'This is your bathroom.' He could have been a hotelier, showing the latest arrival around. 'It's very small, I'm afraid, and the water supply is temperamental. It comes from a cistern up in the hills.'

'Oh, I'm sure it will be fine, thank you, but,' she added awkwardly, 'if it's your room, I'd honestly rather not——'

'Good, that's settled then.' Alex picked up his case, nodded briskly to her and disappeared without another word.

She was still standing staring out of the window when she heard his voice behind her.

'I forgot to ask—would you like something to eat now, or would you rather swim?'

'Oh, I think a swim. That's if you . . .' But as he turned away again, her voice trailed off into silence.

She unpacked her few clothes, hung them in the small wooden wardrobe, then slipped into her bikini. She gazed at herself in the narrow, age-spotted mirror on the wardrobe door, her lips pursed as she studied herself dispassionately, then put on her wrap and began to recomb her dishevelled hair.

She was bending forward, struggling to fix the shiny blonde mass into a disciplined knot, when she heard, 'Keep still,' and from under her lashes she saw Alex's bare, tanned legs right beside her. He caught hold of her hair, gave it one deft twist, then, 'Pins,' he said crisply and, reduced to dumb obedience, she silently handed them up to him.

'There, that should do it.' He stood back, surveying her as impersonally as if she were that hairdressing doll of Poppi's, then, 'Ready?'

When she nodded, he picked up the two beach towels he had slung on to the bed, and she followed him outside again into the scorching early afternoon heat.

'There's a short cut to the beach. We only came the long way round to call on Lefkia.'

He led the way down a track which dived steeply into the pines. Once on the beach, they left their things in the cool blue shadow of the trees and ran down to the sea, across sand which scorched the soles of their feet. Side by side, they plunged into the water and, as if by unspoken agreement, both struck out hard for the deep water beyond the bay.

Selina tired first and turned back. She sat on her towel under the trees, watching him, but then, as he finally slowed and headed back for the shore, she rolled over on to her stomach. She heard his footsteps echoing through the sand under her ear, then little water droplets flicked against her hot skin as he threw himself down beside her.

After a few minutes of silence, though, she heard him straighten up, and when she looked from under the crook of her arm he was sitting cross-legged, vigorously mounding the sand in front of him with both hands. A faint smile tugged at her mouth—what a restless bundle of nervous energy he was.

Little by little, from out of the heap of sand, a griffin was appearing, its mouth drawn back in a lifelike snarl, its scaly body, and the long serpent's tail coiled round on itself. Unable to tear her eyes away, she watched fascinated—though less by the mythical beast which was springing to life under Alex's hands than by those hands themselves. Strong, capable—they were the hands of a man who could succeed at anything he chose. And yet, those long, sensitive fingers, surely they belonged to an artist, a dreamer . . .?

'Do you like it?' He spoke matter-of-factly, without turning his head.

'Oh, yes, it's wonderful.'

He shrugged and sat back on his heels, brushing the sand from his palms. 'I thought it might amuse you.'

'But it's very good,' she insisted. 'Really lifelike.'

'Thank you.' He made a self-mocking bow. 'Actually, I had ideas of being a sculptor when I was young. But with my father dying when I was seventeen, and the Petrides empire waiting—well——' He spread his hands expressively, but then, as if to obviate any sympathy she might be feeling for him, leapt to his feet. 'Now—lunch, I think. I'm starving, if you're not.'

He held out his hand and lifted her effortlessly, then bent to pick up his towel. As she knotted the tie of her wrap, she saw him put his foot on the griffin, ruthlessly twisting it until the creature was just another pile of damp sand.

Back at the house, she insisted on helping prepare the meal, so they worked together in the pine-furnished kitchen, then ate, mostly in companionable silence, out on the veranda. The food was simple—taramasalata, a salad of Greek goat's cheese and big ox-heart tomatoes, a green salad, rough bread, followed by a dish of large juicy figs, the ripeness bursting through their purple skins, and a bowl of apricots, which Alex picked from the old tree growing against the side of the house. He drank retsina, the powerful resinated white wine, but for her he opened a bottle of light, fresh-tasting *aretsinoto*.

As they were eating, Yannis came by, his lethal-looking twelve-bore cradled lovingly across his arm. He was built on the lines of a battleship, with a bull neck and a seamed, weather-beaten face, but he raised Selina's hand to his mouth as delicately as a courtier, shook hands with Alex man to man—not in the least master to servant, she noted—then, after a few words, whistled off the two huge black dogs which had been alternately

sniffing suspiciously at her and fawning on Alex,
and went off down the path.

When they had finished, Alex showed her how
to prepare Greek coffee in the correct way: two
small cups, half-filled with grounds, then water
boiled in a tiny long-handled metal pot and poured
straight into the cups.

'Now, drink that down straight away, while it's
still hot enough to take the hairs off your chest from
the inside!'

He smiled down at her, the new, totally
amicable, undemanding Alex—or rather, she
thought, the old Alex . . .

They swam again, and after another simple meal
they sat outside in the warm dusk, listening to the
small sounds of invisible insects all around them
and watching the moon make a pale pathway of
light across the water below them, tipping all the
tiny ripples with silver.

Then Alex switched on the terrace lights and,
while he engrossed himself in a book, she opened
the beautifully carved wooden display cabinet
which he had found for her and went through the
drawers, admiring the collection of tissue-wrapped
shells, stones and dried seaweed which, he told her,
her grandmother had made when she was a girl.

It was only when she was in bed, watching the
pattern of moonlight as it moved across the wall,
that she realised that she had hardly thought of
Alex's words all day. It was as though they had both
been so much happier, so much more relaxed, now
that he had made his decision, that the tensions of

the present had vanished, giving way to the uncomplicated freedom of the past.

'I am releasing you . . .' The gratitude welled up inside her again. He was letting her go—and without a struggle. She smiled and rolled happily over into sleep.

She woke with a start from a bad dream, which she could not remember at all, and lay sweating. A dull, heavy feeling had settled around her ribs and her throat felt tight. Oh, no, she wasn't going to be ill, was she? She put the back of her hand to her forehead; it was warm, but not abnormally hot, so it must be the dream. Pushing back the sheet, she went through to the tiny bathroom to shower.

Back in the bedroom, she was standing in front of the wardrobe, trying to decide what to wear, when, without warning, the door flew open and Alex came in. She was not in direct line with the door, so he did not see her for a moment, but then, before she could move, or do more than fling her hands up in an instinctive gesture to cover her bare breasts, he had turned his head sharply towards her.

One swift glance had taken in her nakedness, and then he frowned—as though, she thought afterwards, he was displeased with what he saw—and then, with the briefest of apologies, he had gone.

She realised that she had been holding her breath. Now she expelled it and sank down on to the bed. Of course, Alex was just being thoroughly sensible, keeping true to his promise, she knew that. But even so, need he have retreated with quite such obvious eagerness . . .?

The day passed much like the previous one, with swimming, sunbathing, and simple, leisurely meals. Then, in the evening, Alex provided her with another of her grandmother's collections—this time a huge scrapbook of pressed wild flowers—and settled himself again with his book.

But somehow this evening the novelty had worn off for Selina and she just idly flicked through the pages before putting it down abruptly. When Alex glanced up enquiringly, she said hurriedly that she was tired and was going to bed. She half thought that he might try to persuade her to stay, but he only smiled, remarked casually, 'Yes, it's all the swimming, I expect,' and returned to his book.

Tired or not, she did not sleep well, waking several times from that same dream, which again she could not remember, and when she finally roused the heaviness was still there, but had now localised itself into a nagging ache in her chest, while her throat was still dry and tight. Perhaps she ought to tell Alex. But no—he would certainly insist on going back to Tinos immediately, and she didn't want to do that.

In any case, by the time she had showered the pain had eased a little, so she put on her bikini then topped it with white shorts and a peach-coloured voile blouse. She pulled her hair back from her face into a high pony-tail and went through to the kitchen.

Alex was in a navy short-sleeved shirt and beige shorts, and had obviously just showered—the ends of his black, springy hair were curling wetly into his nape, and his shirt was unbuttoned, revealing the damp fuzzy hair on his chest. He was packing food into a wicker basket, which was already half-full, and after adding a bottle of wine he glanced up.

'Morning, Selina.'

'Good morning.' The tightness in her throat made her words sound forced, almost constrained, but he did not appear to notice.

'Get yourself something to eat—Lefkia's brought up some fresh rolls and yogurt—while I finish this. We're taking a picnic today—it's about time I showed you the island.'

After breakfast, he struck off, not in the direction of the sea, but inland up the hill behind the house, and half an hour's walk brought them down to another small cove.

'We'll have a swim first, before we go any further.'

He slid out of his shorts to reveal his black briefs, slung low across his slim hips and powerful thighs. Between the waistband and his tanned midriff there was a narrow line of paler flesh, and Selina, realising all at once that her eyes were riveted to this, hastily dragged them away and began taking her off her own shorts and blouse.

She followed him down the beach and stood watching him, silhouetted against the dazzling blue, then, as he turned to say something to her, their eyes met and locked. Just for one heartbeat he stood where he was, half turned to her, then he swung away abruptly and dived head first into the water.

All the time she was swimming he did not come near her—she could just see his dark head bobbing further out, beyond the cove—and when he eventually returned she was lying on her stomach again, her chin on her arm, but this time he shook out his towel and, placing it with great deliberation several feet away from her, threw himself down on it.

Although neither of them had said anything, Selina sensed that the restful, easy companionship of the past two days had evaporated. She was on edge, and Alex too seemed strained—she could almost hear the tension crackling inside him. Maybe he was thinking that bringing her here, to the island, had been a mistake—that it would have been better to let her go straight away. And perhaps he was right, she thought miserably. If she had told him that she didn't feel well, they could have been halfway to Tinos by now.

She turned her head restlessly and opened her eyes, to find herself staring straight into his brooding, dark blue gaze. Her heart collided painfully with her ribs and she jerked her head away, just as he jumped to his feet, already reaching for his clothes.

'Come on—let's get moving.'

He pulled on his shorts, snatched up the basket and strode off along the beach, leaving her to hurry after him.

The cove ended in a steep, rocky cliff and Selina was just beginning to think that she would not make it to the top when the path levelled out. The land here came to a narrow point, between the bay where they had been and a stretch of jagged coastline. The very edge was covered in grass and creeping thyme, but set back a few yards there was a grove of ancient, stunted oak trees, and among them—Selina gave a gasp of astonishment and swung round to Alex.

'Yes, that's right. It's a temple—at least, it was.'

Wonderingly, she walked across to the tiny ruined building and carefully stepped up on to the cracked circular stone platform. There were just two of the fluted white marble columns, standing at one side and supporting a small piece of the carved pediment. The rest lay in a heap of broken rubble under the trees.

'Its—it's wonderful,' she said slowly.

She looked round to find him watching her.

'Yes, it is, isn't it?' he said, but then turned away and began busily unpacking the picnic hamper, as though he didn't want to have any part of this magic moment. She stared down at him for a few seconds, feeling the bubble of elation prick inside her, then went slowly across to help him.

As they ate in the shade of the trees, propped against the gnarled trunks, though, she could not tear her gaze from the ruined building.

'I've only seen pictures of Delphi,' she said, 'but surely this is like a mini-version of that temple—what's it called?—the *tholos*.'

He smiled briefly. 'We like to think it was designed by the same architect, although this one is supposed to be dedicated to Dionysus—you know, Bacchus, the god of wine. If you look up there, at the top of that column, you can just make out a pattern of vine leaves, and that was his emblem. There's a legend that he and his troop of female groupies stopped off and had one of their bacchanalian orgies right here, on this very spot.'

His dark eyes were still on her, but his face was quite inscrutable as he went on, 'So, you see, your grandmother doesn't just own an island—she has her very own ruined temple too.'

'Yes. That's marvellous.' She looked at him, shining-eyed. 'I never knew. My f— no one's ever told me about all this.'

'And, of course, it will be yours one day.' His voice was expressionless.

'Oh, I—I hadn't thought of that.'

'Well, you'll need to. Not yet, but one day.'

'Yes, I suppose so.'

'It should fetch a good price. Greek islands don't come on the market every day.'

She stared at him aghast. 'Oh, but I could never sell it.'

He shrugged carelessly. 'That's up to you, of course, but Lefkia and Yannis won't be here forever, and you won't have much control over the place when you're two thousand miles away. More salad?'

He held up a plastic bowl, seemingly oblivious

to the maelstrom of emotions that his casual words
had created in her.

'Oh, no, thank you.'

'You haven't had any olives.'

'I don't like them very much.'

'Nonsense. You obviously haven't tasted Tinos
olives. And anyway, it would be a personal insult
to me—as a native of Tinos—for you to leave
without eating some.'

Did he have to go on and on endlessly about her
leaving, she thought resentfully, and did he have to
seem quite so eager to see the back of her?

'Well, I'm sorry,' she snapped, 'but I just don't
like them.'

His brows came down in a thunderous scowl and
for a terrifying moment she thought he was going
to pin her to the grass and force-feed her with every
olive in the bowl, but then he lifted one shoulder
in a tiny shrug.

'OK, suit yourself. But you don't know what
you're missing.'

And he reached forward and helped himself to a
handful.

She sat in silence, watching him eat, then
thought, This is ridiculous. All this beauty and I'm
sulking over a few silly olives. She caught his eye
and gave him a rather shamefaced smile.

'Sorry,' she said. 'I will try one, if you like.'

Alex delicately picked out one olive. 'Open
wide,' he said, and popped it in.

She chewed it round reflectively, then decided
that he was right after all—she rather liked the

salty—no, smoky taste. She spat out the stone and he fed her more, dropping each into her mouth as though she were a baby bird. But she could not help noticing that he took great care never to touch her lips with his fingers.

To finish, Alex placed a bowl containing peaches and bunches of the small, sweet local grapes between them, and peace was restored. Just once, as they reached simultaneously for the same peach, their hands brushed against each other, and he swiftly withdrew his to allow her to take up the fruit.

Alex had opened the bottle of sweet, sparkling wine and she held out her empty glass. 'Can I have some more, please?'

'Well,' he hesitated, 'are you sure? You've had two glasses already, and it's stronger than it looks——'

'Quite sure,' she said firmly. 'After all, if I can't drink wine in the temple of Dionysus . . . '

With a tiny shrug, he refilled her glass and she leaned back against the tree, alternately eating grapes and sipping the wine. Half closing her eyes against the brilliance of the afternoon sun, she saw through the screen of her lashes the trees, the white marble columns, the sea. The mysterious, potent spirit of this place: the colours, the heat, the scent of the thyme crushed by their bodies—and Alex, his nearness, his brown hand resting on the grass beside her. It was all burning into her senses, filling her as though she were this glass of wine. Very deep inside her, she felt something—her Greekness? she wondered confusedly—begin to stir and tremble into life.

Her pony-tail was irritating her, catching on the rough bark. Barely aware now of what she was doing, she pulled the clip off and, impatiently shaking her silvery-blonde hair on to her shoulders, leapt to her feet. As Alex stared up at her, his brows raised, she jumped on to the platform, still clutching her glass, and, without the slightest thought of what she was going to do, launched headlong into the opening speech of Euripedes' *The Bacchae*.

She had almost finished when she realised that Alex had put down his glass and, chin on hand, was watching her with an unsmiling intentness that made her falter.

'You've put me off,' she said belligerently. 'I know the rest of it.'

'I'm sure you do,' he said pacifyingly. 'Your command of Ancient Greek astonishes me—I forgot mine long ago.'

Mollified, she smiled down at him. 'Well, my——' she had been about to say father, but had just enough sense to substitute '—teacher taught me very well.'

She raised her glass to arm's length and slowly tilted it so that the remnants of wine fell on to the marble in a thin golden stream.

'Now what are you doing?'

'Giving a li-libation,' she stumbled slightly over the word, 'to the gods.'

'Hmm, and particularly to Bacchus, I suppose.

Don't forget to make a wish, in return—sacrificing
wine like that, you should certainly get your heart's
desire, as long as you're quite sure you know what
that is.'

She looked down at him sharply, but his face was
quite inscrutable, and as she stepped down from
the plinth he got to his feet.

'I'm going back down for a swim.'

He barely glanced at her and did not even ask if
she wanted to join him.

'Yes, all right. I'll stay here.'

Her voice was small and, quite without warning,
she felt tears pricking at her eyes as, a moment later,
he went off down the steep path. She bit hard on
the tender inside of her mouth to force back the
tears and sat staring at the two marble columns,
impassively watching them move up and down in
front of her in a shimmering blur.

Finally, she roused herself and repacked the
picnic hamper, but the slanting late afternoon
shadows were already falling across the clearing
before she heard the little rattle of loose pebbles
under his feet.

He surveyed her in silence, then said curtly,
'Ready to go?'

'Of course.'

Evading his outstretched hand, she sprang to her
feet and, snatching up the wicker basket, set off
down the steep slope. She could hear him just
behind her and quickened her pace, stumbling
among the rough shale.

She heard him say sharply, 'Be careful,' and half

turned to snap that she was perfectly all right. Next moment, her left foot went down on a rock which twisted away from her and, with a smothered cry, she fell sideways off the path, sliding helplessly down the loose ground until she fetched up against a clump of bushes.

Raging with herself, she lay still for a moment, then Alex had leapt down beside her and was lifting her into his arms.

'Are you OK?' His voice was taut with shock.

'Yes.' At the sight of his face, very pale under the tan, she managed a weak imitation of a smile. 'Just winded, I think. Oh, no, I've dropped the basket. It's——'

'Oh, damn the basket. Are you sure you're all right.'

She eased herself up in his arms, then heard him give a sharp exclamation, and when she looked down she saw blood on her white shorts. Very gently, he eased them up, and they both saw a deep, ugly graze all up her left thigh, blood oozing from a dozen needle-point wounds.

He cursed softly under his breath and she said quickly, hating the white look on his face, 'It doesn't hurt, Alex—honestly.'

'Give it time,' he said grimly. 'I must get you back to the house. Can you stand?'

She scrambled to her feet, then bit her lip against the pain which flared through the leg from ankle to thigh. He must have heard the tiny moan she gave, though, for he put his arm round her, taking her weight on himself.

She looked around her, then wailed, 'Oh, Alex—the basket. It must have fallen right down to the beach. It'll——'

He said something terrible-sounding in Greek, then, 'Shut up about the bloody basket,' and very carefully he began helping her down the path.

It was a slow, painful crawl back to the house. Selina's stubbornness somehow kept her on her feet, and it was only when the house was in sight that she pulled up, wiping away the beads of sweat that had broken out on her forehead.

'Oh, Alex, I'm so sorry. I've ruined today.' Her lips trembled. 'You're right—I'm still a silly b-baby.'

But he snatched her to him. 'Oh, my——'

He broke off and, swinging her up into his arms, carried her the rest of the way and she leaned against him, feeling the touch of his warm skin comfortingly through the thin blouse.

Shouldering open the bedroom door, he laid her carefully down on the bed, then went into the kitchen and came back with a bowl of warm water and a roll of cotton wool. She felt his hand on the zip of her shorts and her whole body tensed.

'Oh, for heaven's sake, Selina,' he said irritably, and when she looked at him she saw that that moment of softness had gone. There was a grimness now about the set of his mouth and lips which frightened her, so she lay back, obediently allowing him to ease down her shorts.

His hands were as gentle as a woman's. She only flinched a couple of times, but then, when he was running his fingers experimentally over her ankle, a little sigh broke from her and his hands stilled instantly.

'Did I hurt you?'

'N-no.'

'Liar.'

For a moment, a smile lightened the sombre lines of his face, then he gave one of her hands a slight squeeze. 'You haven't sprained it, fortunately—it's just a bad twist. I'll put some arnica cream on it, then I'll bandage it up tightly and it should be fine in a couple of days.'

'Thank you. Nik obviously isn't the only doctor in the Petrides family.'

Again, that flicker of a smile, then he began smoothing on the cream. His fingers, so firm yet so sensitive, easing the pain from her and yet, at the same time, sending little charges of electricity sparking from her nerve-ends to every part of her . . .

He made her stay on the bed while he prepared a meal, then she ate sitting up, while he perched uncomfortably in the bamboo chair. She was surprised that she enjoyed the meal so much. In spite of the pain in her leg, it was somehow very pleasant sitting there, not talking much, for Alex seemed rather far away now, almost aloof, but none the less, it was very comforting with him beside her, both of them held in the circle of light from her bedside lamp.

He cleared away the trays then came back in with a carafe of water and a glass. 'In case you need a drink in the night.' He eyed her critically for a moment. 'Bed for you, I think.'

He reached down and began unbuttoning her blouse. This time she knew better than to protest, and allowed him to peel off the blouse, then the bikini, which had dried on her. He took the pink cotton nightie from under her pillow, ordered, 'Lift your arms,' then slid it down over her naked body. The whole action was so—impersonal. Exactly as if he were putting a little child—Poppi, perhaps—to bed . . .

'Oh, just one more thing.'

He picked up from the dressing-table a tissue-wrapped packet which he had also brought in with him and held it out to her. She pulled aside the paper then lifted out the small glass dolphin, arched as though joyously leaping from the waves, and held it up so that the light from her bedside lamp shone through the blue-green glass. She stared at it, a strange pain tugging at her inside.

'It's really lovely, Alex.' She managed to smile at him, but he did not return the smile.

'I was intending to give it to you as a going-away present,' his voice, like his eyes, was totally without expression, 'but I thought it might cheer you up tonight.'

'Oh, yes, thank you. It has.'

But, in fact, far from cheering her up, his words had sent black depression oozing all through her again. She couldn't bear Alex to sense her mood, though, so she bent her head over the dolphin, stroking her thumb across its cold smoothness, then finally set it down on the table.

'Call me if you want anything.' He stood gazing down at her, his face abstracted, as though he hardly saw her, then rested his hand briefly on her forehead. 'Goodnight, Selina *mou*.'

'Goodnight.'

He switched the bedside light off and a moment later the door closed softly behind him. Selina lay open-eyed, staring into the sudden dark, which mirrored the darkness within her.

CHAPTER TEN

THAT same dream. That same dull ache inside when Selina woke next morning. She pushed back the sheet, gingerly touched her thigh, where the ugly graze had already begun to scab over, then flexed her ankle—that seemed much better, too, apart from some stiffness. She'd really been incredibly lucky—this morning, she could be nursing two broken legs, at least.

But then she rolled over, caught sight of the dolphin, and her relief evaporated. *A going-away present . . .*

Alex was not in the kitchen. Perhaps he was still asleep, but as she hesitated she heard a noise outside, and when she went round to the back of the house she found him, spanner in hand, kneeling in front of the large old generator which powered the house.

He did not look amiable: in fact, ill-temper was emanating from him in an almost visible cloud. She hovered in the doorway, then, as he turned and favoured her with a brief scowl, she ventured, 'Is it broken?'

The innocent enquiry seemed to infuriate him even more.

'What amazing powers of perception you have this morning. Of course the bloody thing's broken! Why else would I be up to my elbows in grease?'

He gave the spanner a savage turn then, without looking at her, snarled, 'Oh, go and have your breakfast. And for heaven's sake keep the fridge door closed.'

'Would you like me to go and fetch Yannis?' she asked tentatively.

'What? No, I can manage perfectly well, thank you.'

She stared at him, feeling her own temper beginning to ignite, but then, refusing to allow herself to be frightened off by his ill-humour, she went and stood just behind him.

'Hand me that wrench.'

He gestured with his head and she leapt to obey. As he withdrew one hand from the murky bowels of the generator, he jammed his hand hard against the metal edge and Selina, holding out the tool to him, winced at the flow of Greek expletives. Without turning, he held out his hand impatiently and she gave the tool to him. He went to use it, then withdrew it sharply and hurled it across the yard, striking sparks from the stone floor.

'Oh, for—— Don't you know the difference between a spanner and a wrench?' He shot her another scowl. 'Stupid question. Of course you don't. You can spout Ancient Greek, but you——'

'Oh, shut up!' Selina shrieked at him. She snatched up another tool and threw it down so hard that it bounced up, almost hitting his kneecap. 'Is that it?'

They glowered at each other for a moment, then, 'Yes, it is.'

Taking up the wrench, he turned back to the machine.

Selina backed up against the house wall and stood, arms folded, looking down at him, intently studying this man who was her husband . . . the strong, tanned legs, with their sheen of dark hair . . . then bare torso and back, lean and hard. Her eyes travelled slowly up . . . the endearing way his dark hair turned into his nape . . .

Down one cheek was a long streak of oil where he'd wiped his hand across. She stared at that streak and then at his profile for a long time, as though trying to imprint it on her memory forever. For of course, after these few days, she might never see him again. Would he marry again? The sudden thought was strangely disturbing, but she forced herself to examine it dispassionately—after all, it couldn't matter to her, could it?

Of course he would. A man like Alex would want a wife beside him. Might he, when the ripples from the divorce had settled, marry Cleo? It would be a most suitable match—she was beautiful and rich. Moody, sullen, of course, but surely Alex was the one man in the world to tame her.

'I'll have that spanner now.'

Alex was holding out an imperious hand and automatically she retrieved the tool from where he had hurled it and gave it to him. He muttered something which just might have been 'Thanks' and set to work again.

Cleo and Alex . . . She was already closing her eyes against the images when a vicious pain, as though someone had savagely driven a knife into her, ripped through her guts, so that she almost doubled up. She didn't want Alex to marry Cleo—she didn't want him to marry anyone. Not Cleo, not anyone should have Alex. She couldn't bear it.

In that instant, she finally remembered that recurring nightmare, which each night had flooded back into her and which she had then forgotten on waking. Each time, in that terrible dream, she had been searching for Alex, ever more desperately. Finally, she had seen him, in the far distance at the end of a dark tunnel, but he had only turned, just once, to look at her, then walked away . . . She gave a faint, humourless smile. Her subconscious had known all along what her consciousness had refused to admit.

The truth had hit her at last, knocking every ounce of breath from her body, as though someone had slammed her against this stone wall. She loved Alex—no, she was crazy for him, trembling for him to take her in his arms and love her. But it was too late. She'd clung too long, like a terrified child, to the old, secure relationship. If she hadn't been so blind—so fearful, she would have seen that this wasn't enough any more and that what she wanted was the new relationship he had offered her, where she was no longer a child, but a grown woman—his wife . . .

Alex flicked a switch, and the generator coughed then hummed gently into life. He grinned at her, his irritation apparently forgotten, and began gathering up the tools.

'Sorry I was in such a foul mood. How's your leg?'

'Oh, much better, thanks.' Her voice didn't belong to her.

He went down on his haunches and studied it. 'Yes, it's healing nicely.'

He gently prodded her ankle with his little finger. Those same sparks of electricity went zinging up her leg and he must have felt the slight quiver that went through her for he drew back.

'Sorry. I hurt you.'

'Oh, no, you didn't. That is——' she broke off in confusion, then added almost inaudibly, 'you've got oil on your face.'

He straightened up, holding out his filthy hands. 'Get it off for me. There's a clean handkerchief in my pocket.'

She pulled it out and began dabbing at his cheek, carefully recalling her eyes each time they strayed towards his dark blue ones. He must be aware, surely, of her rapid breathing, the high colour in her cheeks. Any moment, she was going to have to fling down the handkerchief and run.

'Here, let me do it. We'll be here all day.'

He snatched the cloth from her and began scrubbing hard at his face, but then said, 'I'll go and clean myself up properly.'

When he had gone, she leaned against the wall again, feeling the tight ball of misery inside her chest flex and expand a little. Of course, he did not love her, she knew that, but by rejecting him this second time she'd so damaged his fierce pride that now he could not even bear her to touch him. How he must hate her.

When Alex, set-faced, came into the kitchen, she had prepared breakfast and they took their places opposite each other. He reached for the bread and, without a word, began eating. She ladled some of the creamy local yogurt into a bowl and took a large spoonful of dark gold honey. She drizzled it across the top, then, realising that her spoon had somehow formed the letter A in a thin gold thread, she thrust the point into the yogurt and stirred it round and round.

She shot him a covert look, but he was engaged in peeling a peach. Was it really too late? Couldn't she say to him, 'Look Alex, I know I've been the most stupid fool, but——' No, of course she couldn't. He had become so aloof, as though half the time he didn't even see her, that to try and explain would be like bouncing words against a solid wall.

Actions, though . . . The faintest glimmer of an idea stirred in her, and she bent forward so that her swinging hair hid the sudden tell-tale colour in her cheeks.

'Of course, I've only patched it up.' Alex was speaking. 'It really wants some parts from the mainland. But it should last a day or so, which is all we need, anyway.'

'Oh.' Somehow, she kept her voice neutral. 'We'll be going back soon, then?'

He was pushing the peach stone abstractedly round and round his plate. 'With that leg, you can't swim, and you won't even be able to walk far, so I don't see any point in staying, do you?'

'Well, no, I suppose not.'

'We could go today, if you want.'

'*Today*?' Selina's fingers tightened on the spoon until the cold metal cut into her skin. 'But we don't have to go s-so soon, do we?'

He shrugged indifferently. 'OK. We'll see how you are tomorrow. If you want to go to the beach this morning, I'll help you down. We'll take a picnic again, if you like.'

'What?' Her thoughts, given added urgency by his words, had been leap-frogging ahead. 'Oh, yes, I'd like to. And I'll try not to lose the basket this time.'

But he did not return her smile.

She had found the candles—obviously an emergency supply—in a cupboard, and she was just bending over the table lighting them when Alex came up the steps to the veranda. She was screened by the vines which hung down from the wooden lattices, and he did not at first see her.

'Sorry I'm late,' he called, 'but I couldn't get away. Yannis doesn't——'

He stopped dead, taking in the candles, the pretty white flower decorations, and finally, as though reluctantly, his eyes travelled to Selina, standing at the far end of the table, her newly washed hair gleaming against her slender neck, the black jersey dress clinging softly to the feminine curves of her body. Their eyes met, and something vibrated softly in the air between them, so that she felt her pulses quicken with a thrill of half-fearful excitement.

Then he said, in almost his normal voice, 'Yannis doesn't see many people to talk to.'

'That's all right. I've only just finished.'

'I didn't realise this was a formal dress meal.' His voice was back under control now. 'I'll go and change.'

But his eyes were still on her and he did not move. She smoothed down the fabric over her hips, in a barely conscious provocation, then, feeling the clamminess on her palms, thought, Don't blow it now. It's tonight, or never. But she really wasn't sure of what her next move ought to be; maybe she should just relax and let her female instincts take over . . .

'I've just got this last candle to light,' she said and, very deliberately, turned her back to reveal the waist-deep plunge of the dress. She heard his breath hiss softly, then she took up the matches. She was fumbling awkwardly, seemingly unable to strike them when, from just behind her, she heard, 'Here. Let me.'

Alex leaned past her, his bare arm brushing hers, and, removing the matches from her, he lit the candle. He blew out the match, then, taking hold of her left hand, turned it over. The ring glowed softly in the candle-light.

'A moonstone for a moon goddess,' he

murmured. 'Selina the huntress.'

'That's right.' She looked straight at him,
meeting his gaze unfalteringly.

His fingers tightened on hers for an instant, then
he said, 'I'll go and dress.'

The door closed behind him and Selina, her legs
feeling ever so slightly wobbly, sank down into one
of the wicker chairs. The bottle of ouzo stood ready
on the bamboo table beside her. She poured herself
a generous slurp, added water and sat watching
until the liquid turned to a milky cloud, then drank
it down.

When Alex came back, he had changed into a
long-sleeved white shirt, open at the neck, and a
pair of hip-hugging charcoal trousers. He poured
himself a drink then lowered himself into a chair
alongside her and lounged back, his long legs
outstretched, eyeing the table.

'You've gone to a lot of trouble while I've been
away.'

'Well, it *is* our last night.' The words were out
before she could stop them, and she went on brittly,
'I thought if the table looked nice it might distract
you from the cooking.'

'Oh, I'm sure it will be delicious. But, in any
case, it is not only the table which looks beautiful,
Selina *mou*.'

Despite his bantering tone, there was an
intentness in his eyes which even now, when it was
almost too late, made her just for a moment want
to draw back.

But then she smiled at him demurely. 'Thank

you. Now, perhaps you'd like to eat.'

Without a word, Alex drained his drink and they got up, taking their places facing each other at the table. The large platter of hors-d'oeuvre had been the result of a hurried scramble through the fridge—olives, black and green, sliced tomatoes in french dressing, sardines, cucumber sliced wafer-thin in yogurt and *hoummous*. It was delicious, but she could hardly force a single mouthful down her tight throat, and whenever she glanced at Alex he too seemed to be doing no more than toy with a few olives.

'I'll fetch the next course.'

She stood up, clattering the plates together noisily in an effort to break the silent tension that was weaving itself around the table.

'I hope you like *fondue*.' She set down the dish, together with cubes of bread and two skewers. 'It's about the only thing I can make. We had it at school, whenever anyone had a birthday. I remember one time——'

'Shh.'

As Alex gently put his finger on her lips to shush her nervous babbling, she pulled out the chair beside him and slid into it, half afraid that he would hear her heart, leaping under her ribs.

'I'd b-better sit here, then we can have the dish between us.'

His strong, tanned hand lay on the table, inches away from her own, and she was only just able to resist the urge to snatch it up.

'Now, it's years since I had this stuff. How do I

eat it?'

'Oh, it's very easy. Look.'

She held out a skewered cube of bread and, when he took it, put her hands over his. But her grip was so unsteady that she jolted the bread off the skewer, sending it skittering across the table. Their eyes met and held for an instant, then she seized the bottle of white wine.

'Would you like some more?'

Without waiting for his reply, she refilled his glass, but he ignored it and, instead, remarked conversationally, 'You know, Selina, if I didn't know better I might just begin to suspect that you were trying to seduce me.'

'Well.' It came out as a breathy little sigh. Just for a second, his words, coupled with the spell of those marvellous indigo eyes, knocked her completely sideways, so that her heart threatened to stop beating altogether. But then she managed to meet his gaze quite steadily. 'Is it totally unknown for a wife to seduce her own husband, even here in Greece?'

He took her hand and she knew he must be able to feel the pulse at her wrist, leaping and fluttering against his skin, then, very slowly, he pushed back his chair and stood up, pulling her with him. He held her from him at arm's length.

'Selina?'

There was a husky throb in the word, which only the day before would have hoisted panic signals in her brain. But now it set the exhilarating adrenalin racing through her.

'Alex?'

She smiled up at him from under the fringe of her lashes, then very deliberately lifted one hand and brushed it against his warm mouth. He gave a shaky laugh and gathered her into his arms.

'But what about the *fondue*?' she whispered teasingly against his shirt.

'The *fondue* can wait,' he said raggedly. 'Oh, Selina, my beautiful, untamed goddess.'

Gently, he lifted her face up to meet his and she closed her eyes, her mouth greedy for the sweet taste of his. She felt his hands slide down her throat, across her shoulders, taking the folds of her dress with them, then, without loosing her mouth from his, she lifted her arms slightly so that he could free them. One hand slid across her back, splayed warm against her bare flesh so that now she could feel the pulse throbbing in *his* wrist. The other cupped one full breast, the moist palm brushing softly to and fro over the tight swollen centre, until she moved her mouth restlessly against his and her nails dug into his back through the fine cotton shirt.

She sagged against him, then dimly heard him groan against her neck, his voice slurred with urgency, 'No, my sweet—not here.'

Then he had swung her up into his arms and was striding across the veranda and down the passage to his bedroom. He set her on her feet, sliding her down his body slowly, so slowly that she felt his hard maleness against her softness. Kneeling in front of her, he slid the dress past her waist, over her hips and down to her feet, then with infinite

gentleness, her white cotton pants were eased over
her still painful thigh.

His dark face looked remote, almost stern, but
his hands were not quite steady and for one
terrifying moment the old fear surged back. He
must have felt the shiver run through her, for he
glanced up sharply into her face, quickly
straightened up, then took her hand and, turning
them over, kissed both palms.

'Trust me, *agapi mou*. Nothing until you are
ready, I promise.'

Then he picked her up again and laid her gently
on his bed.

It was all but dark in the room, but when he
switched on the bedside light and she saw her
nakedness, pale against the coverlet, she gave a
faint murmur of protest. But he softly brushed his
hand over her mouth to quiet her, then undressed
and came down on to the bed.

She had seen him so often almost like
this—naked apart from the briefest of trunks or
shorts—and yet the 'almost' was everything. He
lay beside her, not touching her, and she let her eyes
trail up the long line of him, stretched taut as a
bowstring. His legs—ankle, knee, up to the hard
lines of his thigh . . .

'Don't be frightened, little one,' Alex whispered.
She looked up at him, wide-eyed, and he gave her
a wry little smile. 'See the power you have over
me.'

And quite suddenly, as he took her into his arms,
all the fears vanished in a rush of passionate love

for him, and she knew that she would never be afraid of him again.

When he lowered his head, gently teasing with his tongue around the throbbing aureole of her breast, she felt—just as she had felt that first day out at the rock—her blood coagulate in her veins, thick and heavy. But this time was so different, and when his possessive hand moved in slow, spiralling caresses down from her breasts, over her stomach and thigh, and into that soft, sweet, secret centre, very deep inside her, at the innermost part of her being, she felt her womanhood stir and wake into life, like a delicate bud quivering then slowly unfolding its petals into a perfect flower.

She sighed softly, then, putting her hand on Alex's thigh, felt the tremors running through his tensed body. He was holding himself in check for her, as he had promised, but the aching love in her needed him. Her fingers tightened on his side and she pulled him towards her, whispering, 'Yes—please, Alex,' when he tried to resist.

She slipped her hand down, a light, prickling touch across his haunch and flank, and, slightly lifting her head, fastened her teeth on his chest in a little nipping bite until, with a groan, he rolled over on to her, his rigid control shattered into fragments. But even now he was very gentle and when, as he pierced her, a tiny sigh was forced from her, he stopped, then very, very slowly eased himself into possession of her, the sword taking possession of its sheath.

He was still for a long moment, savouring her

sweetness, then began the first thrust, his hips
moving against hers. Oh, why had she feared this
moment? She put her arms around him, straining
him to her, and in answer he slid his hands beneath
the curve of her buttocks, lifting her into him to
meet each thrust.

Something was blazing out of control inside
her—it was an incandescent, white-hot flame
which was searing her to the bone, consuming her
with its power, burning her to ashes and
remoulding her to fit its own will.

She cried out Alex, Alex, soundlessly, and heard
it echo in her brain, then he held her, shuddering,
as spasm after spasm of exquisite pain-pleasure
racked her body, until they collapsed, utterly spent,
in each other's arms.

When at last she stirred, the bedside light was still
on and she saw Alex, his head on his arm, watching
her. At the expression in his eyes, and at the
memory of their lovemaking, she blushed scarlet,
but he shook his head.

'No—no regrets, please, Kyria Petrides.'

She smiled at him, 'No regrets, Kyrie Petrides.'

He took both her hands in his and very softly
kissed all ten fingertips, his dark blue eyes fixed on
hers over the arch of their hands. But then, just as
he reached out for her, she gave him a wicked,
slanting look from under her lashes.

'Hey, I've just remembered. I was supposed to
be seducing *you*.'

'In that case, *koukla mou*,' he released his grip

on her and flopped on to his back, his arms outstretched, 'seduce me.'

Shyly at first, but with growing confidence, she ran the flat of her hand down his chest and stomach to his thigh, revelling in the tautening of his muscles under her palm.

This time, there was none of the almost unbearable sensation of being broken on that wheel of fire and then remade. Now, under Alex's skilled tuition, she was beginning to learn the secrets of her own body and of her instinctive responses to his body and his touch. This time, she was all honey, drowning in a river of molten sweetness which was flowing unchecked inside her, sweeping her along to finally leave her, dazed and still half drowned, as that sweet tide at last receded.

It was almost dawn when she woke and, still half asleep, rolled over and came up hard against Alex. He too was stirring and she felt his arms go round her, enfolding her to him.

'Mmm,' she murmured drowsily. 'I want to stay here forever.'

She felt him smile against her cheek.

'We'll see, little one, we'll see. But if you stay, I do.'

'Did you really mean it when you said I could leave, that you were going to set me free?'

'Yes, I meant it.' His voice was very serious now. 'I would have let you go if that was what you wanted. Although, if I am wholly truthful,' there was a quirk of amusement in his voice again now,

'I did have just the faintest hope that this island would work its special magic on you—where my own charms had so abysmally failed.'

'It's special magic—oh, the Bacchanal?'

'Something like that. Although maybe I'd forgotten just how those terrible young maidens treated their unfortunate lovers' bodies once the Bacchanal was over.'

'Ripped them apart in a drunken orgy, you mean? But you needn't worry about that,' she whispered, feeling the exultation surge through her as she let her fingers trace a seductive pattern down his spine. 'I have different plans in mind for your body, *kyrie mou* . . .'

The room was bathed in sunlight when she felt Alex easing himself off the bed.

'Stay there,' he commanded. 'I'll get us some breakfast. We never did finish that *fondue*, and I'm starving, even if you're not.'

She gave him a lazy little cat's smile, then, when he had gone, lay back on the pillows, stretching voluptuously. Her body ached all over, but not with pain—more a delicious throbbing, and when she looked down she could see the tell-tale marks of Alex's fingers on her breasts and thighs. She yawned, stretched again and felt herself drifting away into sleep once more . . .

The sound of voices roused her, she wasn't sure how much later. Men's voices. Yannis? Yes, it must be. But then, a split second later, no, it was Nik. Nik and Alex. She heard Nik's voice speaking rapidly, Alex intervening, and then the door from the kitchen to the passage outside the bedroom was softly closed.

For some reason, that surreptitous movement chilled her. She lay for a few moments longer, then got up, barely aware this time of that ache in her body. The only clothes here were her black dress and pants, still lying abandoned on the floor. She caught them up, tiptoed to her room and slipped on her shorts and a T-shirt, then opened the kitchen door.

Alex and Nik, their faces grave, were at the far end of the room, conversing urgently. They did not at first see her, then Nik caught sight of her as she leaned in the doorway and he waved Alex to silence. She came forward, not apparently on her own legs, but on those of a doll.

'S-something's happened.' Her voice was ice-clear. 'It's Grandmother, isn't it?'

Alex came over to her and took her in his arms, cradling her just as though she were that child again.

'No, not your grandmother. Nik has come to tell us. There has been a phone call from your aunt in England.'

'Daddy! Is he——?' The word stuck to her throat.

'No, my sweet. But he is in hospital in Oxford. He has had a serious heart attack.'

That postcard, with its stark message: 'I am with Alex.' Selina stood motionless, the guilt and self-reproach washing through her, then very carefully she disengaged herself from his arms.

'I must go—today.'

That doll had taken over again, speaking for her, because she had forgotten her lines in this play she was enacting, and when Alex tried to take her hand, she freed it.

'I'll go and pack.' She smiled at Nik, a ghostly smile in her stiff face. 'Thank you for coming to tell me.' And turning round, she went back to her bedroom.

She had almost finished when Alex came in.

'Selina.' He took her by the shoulders and looked down at her, his eyes grave. 'You can't go alone. I shall come with you to England.'

'No, Alex.' She was surprised at the vehemence in her own voice, and she sensed him draw back a little as she went on hurriedly, 'Aunt Grace will be there, so I shan't be on my own, and I think it will be better, just now, if you don't come. You do understand, don't you?'

She looked at him imploringly and her voice trembled, but she fought down the weakness that made her want to break into uncontrollable sobs, and he released his hold on her.

'Very well. But I shall of course come with you to the airport. Nik is staying on here to close up the house for the winter.'

'Yes,' she said, with a small smile, 'the summer's over.'

Back in the kitchen, Nik hugged her.

'Don't look like that, little cousin. They can do wonderful things now. I may have failed my pathology exam three times, but even I know that.'

She smiled obediently at the joke, as she was meant to do, then, as Alex appeared beside them, her case in his hand, she picked up her shoulder-bag and together they walked down to the jetty, to the waiting boat.

CHAPTER ELEVEN

IT WAS starting to rain again. Selina stood in the shelter of a beech tree, watching the raindrops plop into a nearby puddle.

A sudden gust of wind sent the dead brown leaves whisking off the tree; one landed on her shoulder and she brushed it away absently. Autumn. Mrs Crutchley, her father's lugubrious housekeeper, had happily informed her only that morning that winter was knocking on the door, and all the beautiful yellow dahlias in the back garden had been blackened by the frost two nights before . . .

A shout of laughter roused her and, looking across the grass, she saw a couple of students, probably taking a short cut through the park to their flats on the Banbury Road. She was gazing idly at them when—didn't she know them? Yes, the girl had been on the business studies course with her—she'd be in her second year now. She herself hadn't gone back, of course, when the new term began in September . . .

And the man. Surely, it was Ian—she hadn't recognised him at first, maybe because he was in anorak and cord trousers, so different from the shorts and T-shirt he'd been wearing the last time she'd seen him. But, in any case, that last time was part of another, earlier existence, before she had changed from a girl to a woman, before she and

Alex——

Alex! She could feel the familiar, stabbing pain rising in her again, above the dull ache that was always there, the ache that had been with her, day and night, ever since those last tense, unbearable minutes at Mykonos airport . . .

She was pushing open their garden gate when behind her a voice called, 'Excuse me a moment.'

When she swung round, she saw a middle-aged woman, tugging at a stout dachshund on a leash and bearing down on her.

'You must be Selina Carey, Professor Carey's daughter.'

'Yes, that's right,' Selina said cautiously, but, after all, her wedding-ring and the moonstone ring were both in their boxes in her top dressing-table drawer, and it saved a multitude of complications to answer to 'Selina Carey'.

'I'm Jane Pym.' The woman put out a hand, adding, as Selina stared at her, 'Your new neighbour.'

Selina finally roused herself. 'Oh, yes—of course. How do you do?' In fact, as with almost everything these days, she'd barely registered the furniture van arriving the previous Friday. 'I'm so sorry. I should have come round to see if you wanted anything,' she said guiltily.

'Oh, not to worry, my dear. *Down*, Soppy,' as the dog tried to launch itself at Selina's knees.

'Soppy?' she smiled.

'Well, his real name's Sophocles, but it never sounds quite right to shout "Just wait till I catch you, Sophocles" when he runs off.' The woman's face, which was rather thin and severe, softened as she smiled. 'I know it's a ridiculous name—everyone tells me that.'

'Oh, no—I think it suits him.' Selina stooped down to pat the neat, silky head.

'Actually, one of the girls at school christened him.'

'Oh, you're a teacher.'

'I was head of classics at a school in Sussex. But then, well—I was beginning to feel that I wanted more time to myself. To travel, you know, and write—and when an elderly relative whom I scarcely knew, was kind enough to die,' a wicked smile crinkled her eyes, 'and leave me quite a handsome annuity, I decided to retire and come back to Oxford.'

'You lived here before then?'

'I was a student here—oh, many years ago.' Miss Pym shook her head nostalgically. 'I was one of your father's first students. He wasn't *Professor* Carey then, of course—just young Dr Carey. We all adored him, you know—we sat at his feet like worshippers at the oracle.'

A worshipper? Selina stared at her. Could this woman, crisply voiced, and crisply dressed in expensive tweeds and suede brogues, ever in her life have been a young, glowing student? And then she saw the faint flush of almost youthful colour on her cheek, the sparkle in the brown eyes, and thought suddenly, yes, she could.

'That was why, to be honest, when the estate

agent told me who lived next door, I felt I just had to have this house, even though it is far too large for one middle-aged woman and her dog. I—er—I was wondering, that is——' the authoritative teacher's voice all at once sounded tentative '—I would love to meet him again. Is he in?'

'Well, yes, he is,' Selina admitted.

In fact, her father never went out. She had spent anxious days and nights, first with Aunt Grace, then, after she had had to return to her veterinary practice in Cumbria, alone, at the Radcliffe Hospital, but then, when her father had come home, he had frustrated all her and the doctor's attempts to get him back to normal. He had not, of course, returned to his college, but when she'd suggested that perhaps he would like his students to come to visit him, if only for tea and a chat, he had resisted strongly and she had somehow forced down her impatience, her trembling anxiety to return to Alex.

But at least the guilt which had tormented her all the way to Oxford—the fear that his almost-fatal heart attack had been brought on by the shock of her postcard—had vanished in a gust of thankful relief when, two days after her arrival, the card had plopped through the letter-box, having been sent on from his address in the States. Precipitately, she had torn it into a hundred pieces and thrown it into the bin.

She would have to tell her father about herself and Alex soon, of course. After much agonising, terrified of causing a relapse in her father's condition, she had removed her rings and they had stayed in that top drawer. But it simply wasn't fair to Alex—or herself—not to tell him soon . . .

And then there was the dowry—that million pounds. So far, she'd pulled back from a confrontation with her father, but she wasn't going to put it off forever . . .

'It would be so nice to see him again.' She realised that Miss Pym was still speaking. 'I'd like to tell him how much I enjoyed that book of his.'

'Yes—but he's been very ill, you see, and——'

'Oh, I know. I was so sorry to hear about it. Perhaps when he's stronger, then . . .' And Selina smiled vaguely and made her escape.

Once in the house, she stood in the dark hall, slowly taking off her wet clothes. The only sound was the regular ticking of the grandfather clock, and she could feel the smothering claustrophobia enfolding her yet again.

'I'm back, Mrs Crutchley,' she called. 'We'll have tea now, please.'

She went into the sitting-room to find her father beside the fire, a book open on his lap, though he was not reading. He'd been so fidgety since his attack, restless, unable to settle to anything for long.

She was pouring the tea, when that pain hit her again, square under the ribs. She was not surprised—after all, it always did about this time in the evening. All day, she would keep herself very busy: turning out cupboards which were perfectly tidy, wandering aimlessly round the Oxford shops,

cooking—under Mrs Crutchley's expert if
short-tempered guidance, she was becoming quite
a proficient cook—and studying. She had bought
a modern Greek grammar at Blackwell's and
struggled with it whenever her father was resting.
But finally, each evening, she had to wind down
her frenetic activity and then, back came the pain,
the dreary emptiness, the physical hunger for
Alex—for his touch, for his embrace . . .

As she was carrying the tea-tray back to the
kitchen, the telephone rang in the hall. Alex! Surely
it was Alex—this time the joyous lift in her heart
couldn't be lying. But it was Aunt Grace; one of
her routine calls to see how her brother was.

Selina replaced the receiver slowly and stood
staring at it through a haze of tears. She'd been so
sure it was Alex. But then, why should it have
been? For, after the first couple of weeks, when
he'd rung every evening and she'd had to hedge
about her return, his calls had become increasingly
intermittent. And when they did come, he had
been—difficult to put her finger on it—remote,
distant, as though more than just a few thousand
miles lay between them.

Now, on a sudden impulse, she fumbled open the
telephone drawer, and found the slip of paper on
which he had scribbled down the number of his
Athens apartment. With trembling fingers, she
dialled 010-30-1 and then his number. But, yet
again, it was his housekeeper who answered, and
Selina gathered that Kyrios Alexis was away in
Rhodes. Last time it had been Istanbul, the

previous time Rome. It was almost as though—Selina thrust the thought from her, and stood leaning her head against the wall.

Oh, lord, what shall I do? she thought, and heard herself say the words aloud into the silence. She was losing Alex; she was drifting helplessly away from him, and the only link would soon be the few letters she had upstairs, in his strong, upright hand, filled with nothing news about the family, those two rings and a blue-green dolphin.

But there must be a way for her. She closed her eyes, pressing her hands to her temples, and very gradually, out of the darkness, came the faintest flickering of an idea . . .

Next morning at breakfast, she said, 'I've asked someone to tea, Daddy.'

Her father frowned. 'But you know I don't like visitors. I'm not well enough——'

'She's our new neighbour, actually. I rang up last night and invited her. After all,' she went on firmly, 'it's only good manners. And besides, you know her.'

'Oh?'

'She was one of your very first students.' She gave him a teasing smile. 'She told me how they all sat at your feet, worshipping you.'

'Really? Well, I suppose young people always have been very impressionable.' But Selina did not miss the flush of pleasure her words had brought to his cheeks.

'You certainly made quite a hit there, anyway.'

'Who is she?'

'Jane Pym. Fairish hair, tall——'

'Good heavens. Jane Pym! Of course, she was a star pupil of mine, my dear.'

He gave a gentle sigh, his thoughts clearly drifting back to those golden days, long before he met her mother. She glanced across at him, and just for a moment, as he straightened his back, his cheeks still flushed, she saw that young, exciting lecturer again. She came round the table and dropped a kiss on his thinning hair.

'I'll cook some scones later and I'll ask Mrs Crutchley to make that special coffee and walnut gateau you're so fond of.'

'That would be nice, my dear. Oh, and Selina, would you go upstairs and see if that black corduroy jacket of mine needs pressing? It's a little—youthful for me, of course, but I cannot possibly receive visitors in these old flannels . . .'

'But, my dear E.C., you simply must begin work on your sequel to *Aeschylus, the Lost Trilogy*. The world of scholarship has been waiting thirty years for it.'

E.C. . . . Selina stirred the contents of the teapot vigorously, bending forward to hide the involuntary smile, but then, as she refilled the cups, she thought, I needn't have worried—they're so engrossed in their conversation that they wouldn't notice if I sprouted three heads.

'Yes, well, of course, Miss Pym—but that seems far too formal for someone I knew when she was a pretty young girl,—may I call you Jane?' and Selina's alert eyes saw the other woman colour like a teenager. 'I did have every intention of beginning the sequel, after those discoveries I made of the linguistic developments of . . .'

Their voices flowed on and Selina sat back, enjoying her gateau and feeding titbits to Sophocles, who sat curled at her feet like a small teak statuette.

It was very late when at last Miss Pym left. She paused in the hall.

'I've—er—invited your father round to tea tomorrow afternoon. I have a small collection of Greek pottery, left to me some years ago by an archaeologist cousin, and he is most keen to see it. Would you like to come too?'

'Oh, that's very kind of you,' Selina hastily extemporised, 'but I—I'm having my hair done.'

And when Miss Pym had gone, she did a gleeful little tap-dance down the hall.

CHAPTER TWELVE

'DON'T go off to bed just yet, Selina. I'd like to talk to you.'

Her father looked up at her as she put down his beaker of Horlicks. She smiled back at him and sat down in the chair opposite.

'You've been looking so much better, Daddy, these last couple of weeks.'

'Yes, well, we had such an invigorating walk this afternoon across the Cumnor Hills. I often used to take my students there on a Sunday.'

He stirred his drink round and round, then at last, 'Selina, I have something to tell you. It has preyed on my mind for months—in fact, I think it made me ill finally.' He pulled a wry face. 'They say that guilt makes a bad bedfellow.'

'Guilt?' Selina's heartbeat quickened.

'Yes. I want to confess something to you, my dear. All the time that I was lying in hospital it was on my mind . . . You know when you went to Greece——' she gave a start but he did not notice, '——three years ago? Well, when you came back, having been married against your will, I was so angry, and then, just a couple of days later, Alex sent me——'

'No, Daddy, don't.' She could guess the agony this was costing him. 'You see, I——'

'——your dowry, I was very angry over that too,

and I was going to send it back. But it was a very
great deal of money and, well, I'm afraid, in the
end, very wrongly, I used it to purchase this house,
the beautiful furniture I always wanted us to have,
and my Apollo.' His hand crept to the beautiful
marble head beside him, and for a moment he
caressed it. 'And then I lied to you, told you that it
was a bequest from your mother. Oh, it's true, she
did leave a bequest—a considerable sum of money
and jewels—but not to me. It was for you, to inherit
when you are twenty-one. For months I've been
worrying about it—I'd even made provisional
arrangements for us to go back to my college
rooms, sell this house and return the money to
Alexis. That was before . . .'

'Before?' she prompted.

'Before I asked Jane to marry me,' he finished
rapidly. 'I hope you don't mind, my dear.'

'Oh, Daddy,' she knelt on the rug beside him,
'it's the most wonderful news.'

'I shall still sell this house, of course, and repay
my debt, but now I shall move next door. And Jane
is most anxious that you consider it your home, as
well, for as long as you wish.'

'I'm glad you've told me, Daddy.' She took a
deep breath. 'You see, I have something to
tell you, as well . . .'

'. . . So, I couldn't have left you while you were ill,
of course, but now I really want to get back to
Athens—to my husband.'

He took her hand in his. 'My dearest girl, I'm so

happy for you. There was *something* in your
face—even those first few days in the hospital,
when you were so anxious about me—a kind of
suppressed joy. But it's faded in the last weeks.
How selfish I've been. *Yes,*' as she tried to protest.
'There is just one thing, Selina. Your feelings for
Alexis—it is more than just a passing infatuation,
isn't it?'

She saw the shadow in his eyes and said, trying
not quite successfully to smile, 'Oh, no, Daddy, it
isn't infatuation, I promise you.'

It was autumn in Athens, too. As Selina crossed the
little square, in a select suburb of the city, the dead
leaves from the plane trees were gusted round her
feet in little eddies.

But Alex was not at home. His grey-haired
housekeeper showed her into the spacious
top-floor apartment, brought her tea in the large
sitting-room, fussed over her, quite overwhelmed
by the sudden appearance of Kyria Petrides, then
left her.

Selina was beginning to regret the impulse
which had made her choose to land on Alex's
doorstep unannounced, and, leaving the tea
untouched, she prowled restlessly around the
room, picking up each beautiful ornament and
setting it down, theny trying to decipher the titles
of the hundreds of books which spilled over the tall
bookcases on each side of the fireplace.

She caught sight of herself in the gilt mirror
above the mantelshelf and made an involuntary

grimace. She'd been pale when she left Oxford, her tan long since faded, but now the fluttering apprehension which had closed on her the instant she stepped from the lift just outside Alex's door had drained every vestige of pink from her cheeks, so that the only spark of colour in her face was the blue of her eyes. She reached for her make-up bag, then thought, What does it matter? And anyway, my hands are shaking so much that I'll only end up looking like a clown.

Finally, in an effort to soothe her jangling nerves, she knelt up on the squashy cream leather sofa under the window to look down, chin on hands, at the traffic and the people hurrying far below.

She watched for a long time, hoping to see Alex coming across the square, but it was dusk when, without warning, she heard the front door of the apartment open. The door to the sitting-room was ajar, and through the gap she saw him. Barely able to breathe for the suffocating hand that was squeezing her lungs, she stared at him as, unconscious of her presence in the unlit room, he took off the light overcoat he was wearing, hung it up, then stood frowning slightly to himself.

How strained he looked, and there was a weary sag to his shoulders that she had never seen before. More than anything in the world, she longed to run across the room, throw open the door and take him in her arms. But something about him—an aloofness—now, at this final moment, held her motionless.

He picked up his briefcase and walked off down

the passage. Hardly aware of what she was doing, she followed him. A light showed from under a door; she opened it and stood in the doorway.

Alex was sitting at a desk, his case already open in front of him, the papers which he was shuffling through scattered across it. He had been wearing a grey three-piece suit, but he had thrown the jacket across a chair and was working in his waistcoat and white shirt and tie.

This was a different Alex—the Alexis Petrides who was the hard, powerful boss of a huge business empire—and she was all at once overcome with paralysing shyness. Her hand went to her throat, fidgeting with the gold chain she was wearing, and he caught the slight movement. He swivelled round, saw her and went very still.

'Selina.'

She forced her legs to advance a few paces over the deep-pile carpet.

'H-hello, Alex.'

But he made no effort to get up. Without taking his eyes off her, he said, 'How long are you here for?'

The wintry coldness in his voice and eyes froze her to the bone, but she forced her stiff lips into some sort of smile.

'How long do you want me to stay?'

'Do I have any say in the matter?'

She stared at him, her eyes blank with hurt. And yet, this was exactly how she had feared it would be. The gulf that had grown between them during the weeks of separation was still there, even now that she had returned. Instinctively, she knew that *she* would have to be the one to reach out to *him*. Drawing in a long, unsteady breath, she crossed the room and stood looking down at him.

'I've come for as long as you like, Alex. But if you don't——' she had been going to say 'love me', but, after all, he had never said that he loved her, and her mind shied away from that ultimate test, so instead she made it '——want me to stay, I can always go . . .'

Still he made no move, just sat staring at her, one hand toying with his pen, and the despair rose in her. How could she ever break through to him? But almost before the question had taken shape in her mind, she heard herself say huskily, 'When we were on the island, you told me that you wanted my spirit, my mind, my soul. Well,' she lifted her arms slightly from her sides in a telling little gesture, 'here I am.'

Even as she gave him a tremulous little smile, Alex leapt to his feet, sending the papers flying in all directions.

'Oh, my darling girl, I was so afraid that——' was all he could manage, then he gathered her to him, his cheek against her hair, and they stood there, locked in each other's arms, for an endless time.

Behind them, the door opened and the housekeeper poked her head in to announce that dinner was ready, then beat a swift retreat.

'Come on,' Alex whispered, gently putting her away from him. 'You must be hungry, and besides, Katia is very jealous of her reputation as one of the

best private cooks in Athens, and I don't want to
offend her.' He gave her a warm, teasing smile
which made her insides flutter. 'I'd hate to have to
live on *fondue* for evermore.' But in fact they
managed to get down hardly any food, for they
were too busy devouring each other with their eyes
to be hungry for much else.

After dinner, he carried a tray of coffee into the
sitting-room and Selina sat on a shaggy wool rug
in front of the log fire, leaning back comfortably
against his knees as he lifted strands of her hair,
letting the firelight flicker red-gold on them.

'Oh, Selina,' he murmured, 'I had almost begun
to believe that you would never come back to me.'

'Is that why you were so—cool on the phone,
and then were never there?'

'Well, I have been away a great deal, sorting out
some business problems. But yes, I think I was
really struggling to school myself to do without
you, if it came to it, for the rest of my life. You see,
I was so fearful that, just as your mother had
pressurised you to act against your will, so you
would allow your father to persuade you not to
return to me.'

'But it's quite different now, Alex.' She turned
and looked at him. 'I was a child then—and I'm
not a child now, am I?'

'No, you are not.' His eyes were sombre black
in the fire glow. 'You are a very beautiful, very
desirable young woman. But, when you'd gone, I
really began to wonder if it wasn't just the island's
magic which had worked on you, and once you

were free of its spell . . .'

He really did need her reassurance and, somehow, she must lighten the dark mood which had fallen on him again. She put up a finger to ease the harsh line between his brows and said softly, 'If it was magic, Alex, it's still working.'

'Oh, my darling.'

As his hands slid from her hair to cup her face, she very deliberately began to unknot his tie. But then her fingers stilled and she gave a little pout.

'Oh, Alex, do you realise you've never told me you love me?'

'Never told you——?' he almost shouted at her. 'You little wretch, what the hell do you think I——? Hasn't my every word, my every action told you that I'm crazy about you?'

He bent and kissed her on the eyelids, then said against her mouth, 'Selina *mou, s'agapo*, I love you.'

'And I *s'agapo* you,' she whispered.

She felt him make a face. 'Excruciating grammar, but I think I get the message.'

And he slid down on to the rug beside her . . .

The fire had burned low. Alex threw on more logs and she lay back, curled against him, her hair spread in a silk curtain across his chest, watching the firelight and shadows make patterns on their bodies.

'You know, *koukla mou*,' he lifted her hand and kissed it, 'I've loved you for a long time. I picked you for myself when you were sixteen and I was utterly determined that no one else would have you. Although she was overjoyed for us to marry, it was not your mother's idea, but mine. I asked her for your hand, but we agreed that it was better for you to think that it was only her and your grandmother's wish. Even though you already had the body of a woman, you were still a child, and I was desperately afraid that I would frighten you off.' He gave her a rueful smile. 'Which I did anyway. I think you saw me, not as your protector, but as the biggest threat of all.'

'But now I've come back, and I shall never go away again, I promise.' She breathed a luxurious sigh.

'What's the matter?'

'Oh, I was just thinking—loving you, living with you, for years and years and years. Seeing you get old.'

'Many thanks,' he said drily.

'You know what I mean.' She caressed his cheek with the tips of her fingers. 'Oh, Alex, you've got a grey hair. Keep still. Look.' She held it up. 'No, it's white.'

He shook his head at her. 'My darling, having known you for as long as I have, I am only astonished that I have a hair left on my head, white or otherwise.'

He dropped a kiss on her nose, then got to his feet. 'Stay there.'

When he came back, he was wearing a navy bath robe and was carrying an enormous sheepskin wrap, in which he enfolded her.

'Come. I want you to see the view.'

He pulled back the heavy curtains at the far end of the room and led her out on to the terrace. At their feet was a carpet of lights, all of Athens unrolled before them as far as Piraeus, and beyond was the blackness of the sea. And over there—Selina's breath caught in her throat—was the Acropolis, floodlit and floating against the dark violet sky like the bones of a sun-bleached ship.

'Oh, Alex, it's so beautiful.'

She turned into his arms to meet his lips, and felt the desire ignite in her again, leaping to meet his. They clung together, their lips joined in an endless kiss, each shaken by the storm of feeling which had swept them up.

A chill wind was rising. She shivered and Alex tightened his hold on her, drawing her into the shelter of his body. In the darkness, Selina smiled. The golden, magical summer of her growing up was over, but she could let it go without regret. There would be so many other summers.

HARLEQUIN
Romance®

Coming Next Month

#3121 NO ANGEL Jeanne Allan
When Elizabeth saves Andrew T. Harcourt's life, she doesn't expect her own to be
turned upside down. She's far too busy for love—which is just as well, since
Andrew apparently doesn't have marriage on his mind.

#3122 ROMANTIC NOTIONS Roz Denny
She's an ex-model running a lingerie store; he's a one-time hockey great who
disapproves of female vanity. They fall in love, but does their love have a chance?
Especially with two teenagers and a glamorous ex-wife to complicate things
even more....

#3123 FIRM COMMITMENT Kate Denton
Architect Ben Weston would do anything for his four-year-old daughter, give her
anything she wanted. Does that include providing her with the mommy of her
choice—his newest employee, Anne Marshall?

#3124 PRETENCE OF LOVE Carol Gregor
Bella Latham is having trouble playing two roles: she has a part in Luke Retford's
film, and she's also pretending to be her twin sister, Mandy, whom Luke had really
hired. But she thinks her masquerade is working—if she can only keep her distance
from Luke.

#3125 LIGHTNING'S LADY Valerie Parv
In the midst of deep unhappiness, Jenny also finds herself pregnant. She heads for
the opal mine her uncle had left her—only to find it really belongs to local grazier
Lachlan Frost. When Lachlan offers marriage, Jenny is stunned....

#3126 A FIRST TIME FOR EVERYTHING Jessica Steele
Harlequin Romance's next First Class destination finds Josslyn accepting a sudden
assignment to Egypt. The job is a delightful surprise. If only she could say the same
of her autocratic new boss, Thane Addison. To say the least, they just don't hit
it off...!

Available in May wherever paperback books are sold, or through
Harlequin Reader Service:

In the U.S.
P.O. Box 1397
Buffalo, N.Y.
14240-1397

In Canada
P.O. Box 603
Fort Erie, Ontario
L2A 5X3

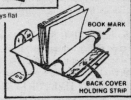